To Love Violets
For Their Thorns

Praise for *Freyja's Daughter*

"[Sullivan] builds a rich version of our world with an easily recognizable Seattle setting. With clever wit, she crafts a battle between Wild Women and Hunters that will inspire readers to fight the patriarchy."—*Publishers Weekly*

"A promising debut from Rachel [Sullivan], *Freyja's Daughter* is an immersive urban fantasy novel with a satisfying feminist theme. Minor conflicts and tensions interplay with the main plot to lead the reader to a thrilling denouement. *Freyja's Daughter* is a rare treat for urban fantasy fans."—*Readers' Favorite Book Reviews*

"Ms. [Sullivan] does an amazing job of giving each of these tribes of women (huldras, mermaids, succubae, rusalki, and harpies) different traits and building background. Faline, the main character, is a huldra and a wild one at that! This book is her self-discovery journey. She gets into some trouble, has some adventure, and above all learns what makes her different! I recommend this debut novel from Ms. [Sullivan] for anyone who loves paranormal romance or even just paranormal at all. I was enraptured from the beginning!!"—*Nerd Girl Official*

"A female bounty hunter with hidden powers and a low lying buzz of chemistry with the cop she interacts with had me pulled in. With an unexpectedly good storyline and a premise that reminds me of authors like Ilona Andrews and Nalini Singh, I was wildly entertained with fantasy creatures walking among us, living for the night, and saving the day. *Freyja's Daughter* has strong female characters, captivating content, and Rachel [Sullivan] shows a talent for writing and content that I can totally see a fan base growing from. I am looking forward to more from this author."—*KT Book Reviews*

"Strong characters. Smart writing. The most fun I've had between the pages in a long time! [Sullivan]'s debut is not to be missed!"—*New York Times bestselling author Wendy Higgins*

"In this wickedly smart must-read debut novel, strong women warriors based on familiar mythologies and folktales band together to take down the patriarchy. Rachel [Sullivan]'s compelling voice, unique worldbuilding, and enchanting characters makes her my newest one-click author."—*Asa Maria Bradley, Award-Winning author and Double RITA Finalist of the Viking Warriors series*

"*Freyja's Daughter*, [Sullivan]'s first book in her Wild Women's series, makes you want to binge the series all at once. Welcome to the entertaining, feminist, and inclusive world of Huldras, Mermaids, Rusalki, and other mythical women—a world you won't want to leave."—*Ivelisse Rodriguez, author of Love War Stories*

"[Sullivan] explodes onto the scene bringing her ideals of feminism and diversity with her. Strong female characters and world building collide leaving the reader breathless and eager for more."—*Samantha Heuwagen, author of Dawn Among The Stars*

By the Author

Freyja's Daughter

Lilith's Children

Ishtar's Legacy

Some Kind of Twisted Love

Some Kind of Pure Obsession

The Hunter and Her Witch

To Love Violets for Their Thorns

Visit us at www.boldstrokesbooks.com

TO LOVE VIOLETS FOR THEIR THORNS

by

Rachel Sullivan

2026

TO LOVE VIOLETS FOR THEIR THORNS

ISBN 13: 978-1-63679-928-5

THIS TRADE PAPERBACK ORIGINAL IS PUBLISHED BY
BOLD STROKES BOOKS, INC.
P.O. BOX 249
VALLEY FALLS, NY 12185

FIRST EDITION: FEBRUARY 2026

CREDITS
EDITOR: RUTH STERNGLANTZ
PRODUCTION DESIGN: STACIA SEAMAN
COVER DESIGN BY TAMMY SEIDICK

To my readers,
Whether you've run alongside folkloric warrior women,
swum with man-eating sirens, fallen in love with powerful witches,
or are just now joining my mind's adventures:
Thank you for trusting me with your time, your imagination,
and your emotions.
Happy Reading

Chapter One

Sonia

Windshield wipers set to full blast, I eased my truck from the hospital's staff parking garage and onto the road. Rain pelted the glass, fracturing traffic lights to streak across my view of the city of Spokane, Washington.

Located in eastern Washington, twenty minutes from the Idaho border, Spokane's downtown was built during the decades before and after the turn of the twentieth century, and it showed. Our big-little city was known worldwide for our annual basketball competition, Hoopfest, and our annual 12K run, Bloomsday, as well as two popular private universities.

I worked as a registered nurse in the emergency department of Sacred Heart, a hospital located on South Hill, with sprawling views of the city below and beyond. Nursing hadn't been my dream job, but I wasn't the dream job sort. Healing people fulfilled me, taking lead in chaotic situations gave me purpose, and Sacred Heart paid my bills.

Given the chance to sit at home alone with my thoughts on my parents' wedding anniversary, versus spending the day on my feet, dealing with the problems of others, I took the latter. Not that I would have spent today alone if I didn't go in to work. My fearless foursome would have made sure of that.

I smiled, thankful to have them, my group of friends. Tonight, we were meeting for dinner at a favorite seafood restaurant of ours.

Living in Spokane meant culture took a while to reach us, as did food and fashion trends. Finally, we had a restaurant that served seafood boils.

When my mom and I chatted last, I had told her about my plans to meet up with my friends tonight, and she reminded me our little city was also getting hot pot and Korean barbecue soon. Our regular trips to Seattle to stock up on ingredients from much fresher and larger Asian markets always included meals at restaurants we couldn't get in Spokane. While I doubted the authenticity of the new restaurants coming, I hoped their arrival would bring familiar meals that much closer to home for my mom and me.

Illuminated shop windows blurred into puddles of color dripping from my driver's side window. Pulling into the crowded parking lot, I spotted two friends' cars and parked beside one of them. In our group text today, carpooling plans were made. From the looks of it, I was the last to arrive.

"No scrubs, huh?" someone said when they all stood at the large, corner booth to welcome me in.

"Gross," I answered, shaking my head and hugging each of them, one at a time.

They knew how I felt about food and hospital germs, and particularly the two together. Which was why they razzed me about it. I would rather be late because of taking the time to make myself presentable. A fresh new hoodie, clean loose jeans, and a spritz of cologne—all items I regularly kept in my locker at work—made a world of difference.

"How did it go today?" Stacy asked once we got settled.

Before I had the chance to answer, our waiter deposited waters on our table and hovered with a notepad in hand. We gave our orders. Once he left, I answered Stacy's question.

"I'm glad I didn't stay home," I started. A flush of emotion shifted in the pit of my stomach, where it had rested all day, and rose up my torso, into my neck. I cleared my throat. "I think today went as good as it could, considering."

Stacy gave a slow, empathetic nod. "Have you spoken with your mom?"

I took a sip of water. "Last night, yes. This morning, no. It's hit or miss when she's on a cruise."

Today, a year ago, was my parents' first wedding anniversary apart. My mom and I had spent the day mourning our shared loss—my dad and her husband. Since then, she'd decided to spend their future wedding anniversaries visiting their bucket list locations. This year, she was enjoying a Rhine river cruise with her sister and my dad's sister. A girls' trip to celebrate a love so pure, not even the darkness of death's shroud held the power to smother it indefinitely.

My dad still lived in our memories, our photos—in the way I ground my teeth when I was stressed, the dimple in my left cheek when I smiled, and in so many ways I was still realizing. We were transitioning from experiencing my dad physically, in the flesh, to other, less obvious ways, like seeing his sparkle in his sister's eyes.

From beyond the grave, the love my parents nourished over the years became its own immortal being. My whole life, I wanted a love like that. A strong, steady, and secure love. The unwavering type, no matter the storms on the horizon.

The kind of love that would bring your wife and sister together in your memory, long after you'd left the world.

When he lived, it was my dad who liked to make a spectacle out of how much he loved his wife. He was the king of grand gestures and romantic toasts. It wasn't until after he died, though, that I got the chance to witness the other half of their love—my mom's quiet and unending devotion, like stems holding up colorful petals.

I eyed my three friends, each staring back. "What?" I asked.

I could have been assuming the worst, and who would have blamed me? Rough days had a way of getting worse. Days like today, when emotional exhaustion sapped my strength to fight off the darker thoughts, I had a tendency to assume the worst.

Three sets of eyes shamelessly studied me. "Why does it look like you all know something I don't?" I groaned and shook my head. "You've got hot gossip." I knew those expressions, juicy news to share with a dollop of pity. "If it's about *her*, like I said, I don't want to know. Otherwise, I can handle it."

I took a deep breath to steady my heart, my beats closer together and growing more rapid. It had been a while since anyone mentioned my ex's name in my presence, so I felt the need to prepare myself.

"How are you doing on vacation time from work?" Jenn asked.

I cocked my head, confused. "Why?" What did that have to do with anything?

"What about by this summer?" Alex asked. "You think you'll have a few weeks banked up?"

The three of them laughed to themselves. My panicked heartbeats sputtered to a slower pace in relief. Their secret had nothing to with my past.

"Okay, so I didn't have *that* good a day," I said, reminding them I was putting a happy face on and couldn't for much longer. I wasn't in the mood to feel like the butt of anyone's jokes.

Stacy touched my bicep from beside me in the booth. "We did a thing," she said. "A good thing. For you."

I shook my head. "Then why does it sound like the opposite of good?"

"Because it's not something you'd normally do," she answered, and then added, "more like it's totally out of your comfort zone. We think it's what's best for you."

I sighed and let my back sink into the cushions behind me. After my dad died, and the initial shock passed, my life felt like a daily dose of discomfort. Nothing stayed the same. What would have been happy moments before—hugs, laughter, connection—were now instances tainted by loss. Even areas I used to find fulfillment in now reminded me of a special kind of pain living below the surface of hugs, laughter, and connection. A pain that took rather than gave, like a void on the verge of swallowing me up.

In the early days, I clung tightly to the hope of *normal* returning, like the clouds would magically part one morning and all my old beliefs and understandings about the world would be reinstated. Normal and comfort would be restored.

But that wasn't how life worked. If spending my years since college working in the emergency department hadn't already taught me this lesson, losing my dad did. People were born. People got sick. And people died. The only consistent was change. Normalcy was a lie we told ourself to get through the chaos, the light at the end of the tunnel that turned out to be merely a figment of our imagination. Despite what I knew, subconsciously I yearned for normal, for comfort. "Getting out of my comfort zone is the opposite of what's best for me right now," I reminded my friends. Routines, habits, calm, and stability were my current goals to support my frayed mental health. Not playing willy-nilly outside my comfort zone.

I thought to add my inner dialogue, to drive the point home. "I don't even know if I really have a comfort zone since his death." Home, work, and my house were not comfort zones. They were bunkers I hid within while bombs of unknowing and missiles of doubting my reality fractured the foundation of knowing my parents would always be my support.

Death had a way of deleting *always* and *never* from a person's vocabulary. The reminder put a damper on my already less than jovial mood.

I wondered if I shouldn't have come out tonight. Maybe I should have just gone home from work, taken a scalding shower, crawled into bed with Harriet, my dog, and watched reality dating shows until we fell asleep. The light-hearted episodes filled with other people's trivial drama brought me comfort. No one was dying or getting an earth-shattering prognosis or any other of life's litany of blindsiding possibilities. Their worst-case scenarios were strangers disliking them. It felt safe.

"You need hope right now," Stacy declared. Her brown eyes focused on mine, locking me in her knowing gaze.

We had grown up together, attended all the same schools. Our moms were close friends who met when we were little, at the one tiny Korean church service in town. Relationships in my mom's side of the family had always been strained. I could count on one hand how many times I met her family of origin growing up. Her little church group became her family, even after she left the faith and churches altogether. In a way, Stacy felt more like a cousin than a friend.

"You're doing so well in your healing," she said. "And we

know you couldn't go with your mom this year because of your leave time, but still, Sonia, you need to live too. Not just your mom. She's creating her new normal—you should too."

I squelched my knee-jerk reaction to disagree when a raw hurt of mine suffered a blow. My friend group had been there for me through it all. My dad's diagnosis and death broke me. Losing Elly right afterward took me to a low I couldn't have imagined existed. My fearsome foursome didn't skirt around my sadness. They didn't demand I don a smiley mask for their comfort. They crawled into the hole with me. Especially Stacy, who, at the deepest point in my grief, brought me dinner nightly for over a week. Sometimes her deliveries included comfort dishes her mom made for me, like oi muchim—marinated cucumbers—and grilled beef galbi.

Of course I needed to start living again. Everyone close enough to know my private life agreed. Actually doing the thing was where I hit a snag.

When life changed in the blink of an eye, how did you change it back? How did you know you *wanted* to change it back? And was it even worth it when another huge life-altering event could throw me back on my ass?

"Learning a new normal takes time," I reminded them, quoting the grief counselor I saw the first year after my dad's passing.

"And intention," Stacy countered, also quoting the grief counselor. During the time she brought dinner nightly, I had been seeing the grief counselor twice a week and often unpacked our sessions while picking at my food.

In the middle of our favorite local seafood restaurant, a quiet stillness settled upon our table like a bubble of awkwardness. Or maybe that was just how I felt. This topic belonged on my couch in the privacy of my home. Not in public.

Still, I tried not to let that be the focus of my thoughts. These were my close friends, who had proven themselves over the years and through difficulties. And they were worried. I couldn't and wouldn't fault them for caring about me.

"We've been over this," I said, my agitation softening to reveal exhaustion. "Dating apps don't work for me. If I'm going to start something real, it needs to start real."

Stacy's eyes flashed. She chewed her bottom lip as the corner of her mouth rose. I'd known her long enough to notice the signs when an idea of hers rose to the surface. Before I could ask about this new idea, she said, "Funny you should use that word, *real*."

"Here we are," our waiter said as he strode up to our table with his arms full. He placed our food and cups of melted butter on the table and reminded us how to best enjoy the bagged seafood boil before asking if we needed anything and bustling off to the next task.

Buttery, garlicky steam danced across our table with hints of creole spices. Rain slinked down the window beside us, skewing the passing cars and streetlights in the night.

"Why is it funny I should use that word?" I asked, once everyone began eating and I was prepared enough to hear the answer.

Stacy swallowed her bite and sipped her soda before answering. "That for you, a connection needs to start real." She broke our eye contact to locate her straw for another drink of soda.

"I don't know why you guys are in such a hurry to get me coupled off," I muttered. Only one of them was in a committed romantic relationship.

"That's not the point," Stacy said. She cracked a crab leg and set the metal cracker onto her plate to make quick work of releasing the meat from its confines.

"You deserve to smile again," Jenn said, from the other side of Stacy. "The kind of smile new and exciting experiences can give. And maybe even come back with an epiphany or two. We'd love to see a new pep in your step."

"Come back from where?" I asked, suddenly worried about what this group of women were capable of when they put their minds together. "What kind of trip did you arrange for us? Because I could probably go for a few days in Vegas, lounging by the pool, out of this cold weather."

Stacy turned her whole body to face me. "I'm glad to hear

you're wanting sun rays and poolsides. We signed you up to go on a trip to Spain during their Pride." Her last sentence fell out of her mouth quickly, one word on top of the other.

"Wait," I said, frozen in place, my hands hovering over the bag of food on my plate. "Why?"

Uncertainty thrummed wildly in my chest.

"It's the trip your dad and you never got to take," Stacy said, as though she'd cracked the code of how to get my normal back. I didn't have it in me to tell her I wasn't sure it existed anymore.

It was all she needed to say before a breeze of memories flowed into my mind. I had shared that memory with them during last Pride season, hadn't I. Over one of the many crying couch sessions in my living room.

The thrumming of my heart slowed to a heavy ache.

My dad had grown up with a close connection to his gay uncle, one that ultimately inspired him to pursue a law degree, to fight in defense of human rights. He was the biggest proponent of love I ever met. And my biggest ally.

During his lifelong pursuit of justice, he gathered information about countries and cultures he thought led the way in celebrating diversity. People we could learn from. Every now and again, out of nowhere, he would share a recently acquired fact. Madrid's weeklong Pride was among the longest and most celebratory in the world, one he planned on taking me to experience one day.

"But why?" I asked again, then clarified, "Why now?"

Stacy exhaled.

"What?"

"I'm just gonna come out with it," she said.

"I wish you would," I countered.

In my peripheral vision, I caught the restaurant door swing open with a woman's laugh. My eyes darted toward the sound. I had gone more than a year without accidently running into her. It would be my luck if that streak broke tonight.

"There's a new sapphic dating reality TV show, and we signed you up, please don't be mad," Stacy said, all in one breath.

My gaze shot back to her. I couldn't help it—a defensive anger ignited behind my eyes. I placed my clenched hands on my lap, out of view, and thought to grab my bag of seafood and walk out. Finish it at home, if my appetite decided to return.

How the hell did they think this would be something I'd be interested in?

Stacy put her hands up. "It's not like other dating shows. They focus on personal growth and empowerment. And I see your face, Sonia. Not growth, as in the bawling on TV kind. At least that's not how it sounds. They're trying to change reality TV, use it for good."

Words failed to come to mind. I only stared, my tightly clenched hands in my lap.

Stacy continued, as though she was selling me on an idea I didn't want. Which was exactly what was happening. "A free, all expenses paid vacation to Spain. You'll stay in a huge villa with other women and be a part of Madrid Pride. It's a once in a lifetime chance, and we couldn't let it pass you by without throwing your name into the hat. It's everything you and your dad talked about, and you love these kinds of shows."

"This summer?" I asked.

My three friends nodded.

Their responses helped me to breathe a little easier. "Well, then I wasn't chosen because they would have already started planning." I couldn't help but stalk my favorite show contestants on social media, and they said they'd known many months ahead of filming that they'd been chosen. "And also, I do love to watch those shows…from the privacy of my bed," I clarified. "With Harriet snoring beside me."

"So…" Stacy chewed her lip during a long pause. "You *were* chosen. All you have to do is confirm it with them and put in for vacation with your job."

Air rushed from my lungs, and I coughed a reply. "Oh God. Are you serious?"

Stacy nodded. "It's called *The Sapphic Bacheloress*." She paused to smile. "It's not like the other dating shows. Even in their name."

I scoffed and shook my head. "Is *bacheloress* even a word?"

Or were they slapping a new label on an old product, promising something they couldn't deliver?

"It's actually a traditional word used for single women. I googled it," Alex advocated as she worked to dislodge meat from a crab claw. "It used to be a negative term until a French novel came out in the 1920s about an independent bacheloress, painting the single woman in a more mysterious light. It's like the show's doing the same, taking back feminine-specific terms and breathing new life into them. I'm a fan of the idea. Especially for a sapphic dating show. They even have purple flowers on all their promotional stuff. It looks classy."

I shifted uncomfortably in place, pulled my hands from my lap, and pressed my palms to the table to steady myself. "I'm not ready to date," I admitted, without an ounce of shame, "let alone try to date as a sad sack in front of the world."

"You're not a sad sack," Stacy scoffed.

"Dip your toes in the dating pool in gorgeous Madrid, then if you want, date someone local once you're back home," Jenn offered. "We figured maybe a romantic vacation sort of situation would reignite that part of you. Put the spark back in your eyes."

I loosened up enough to pop a boiled and seasoned potato chunk into my mouth and thought while I chewed. Not because I felt anything close to hunger. It just gave me a chance to think. I liked surprises, but not ones that included a litany of unknowns and never-befores.

On top of that, there was a lot more to consider than how much vacation time I'd accrued at work. I would need to find a dog sitter and a house sitter. On impulse, the other day at the grocery store I bought a dahlia bulb to plant this May. Who would water my grass and recently potted dahlia during Spokane's peak summer heat? Who would make sure Harriet's special summer pug needs were taken seriously?

When I started wondering if I would need to update my passport before the summer, I stopped myself. "I'll think about it," was all I said.

"Great," Stacy said with a warm smile. "I'll forward you the next steps email they sent me."

I only gave a single nod and pulled a hot deveined shrimp from the buttery bag. My friends smiled triumphantly. Alex changed the topic, and I followed along, grateful to no longer be center stage of their conversation.

The familiar laugh I had noticed earlier pierced through my thoughts again, and I turned to find its source. Not *her*. It sounded so much like her, though. Enough to excite and terrify me with the possibility of her nearness.

I missed Elly's laugh most of all. The way it seemed to spring from a well deep in her soul and rise like joy-filled bubbles, popping to share with anyone lucky enough to bring it out of her.

My focus dropped back to my food as my tablemates chatted about planning a movie night. Absently following a stream of rain as it wound down the window nearest me, I looked forward to dinner being over, the whole day coming to an end, when I could shut myself into the privacy of my truck and let the tears flow.

Because, in my mind, for the longest time, love equaled Elly. In the same way my dad equaled my best friend and biggest ally. Having to come to terms with the fact that I no longer had my best friend and biggest ally nearly broke me.

Was I strong enough to step into a reality where Elly didn't equal love?

Chapter Two

Elly

Despite the two hours I had to kill before my next flight, I had to hurry to see *Circling* in Terminal D and get back in time to wait at my next gate. I couldn't risk missing two flights in a row. But I also couldn't pass up the opportunity to walk the glass labyrinth art installation in the middle of a busy international airport. A moment of grounding calm in the center of chaos sounded about right.

My phone dinged in my purse and my dog Rowdy popped into my mind, stealing my attention from the busyness of Dallas Fort Worth International Airport.

Hoping for a new Rowdy update from my friend caring for him, I rustled through my purse to find my phone while also trying to walk straight and not into people. It was just a random marketing text, though, not a new Rowdy pic. I looked again at the picture my friend had sent before I boarded in Spokane—Rowdy snuggled up in his bed with his toy. I smiled at my phone, happy to see a familiar face in his wrinkly snout and adorably round brown eyes.

Growing up in a family that took pride in what they believed to be familial culture, and what I now knew to be undiagnosed mental illness, gave me major rejection sensitivities and taught me to trust animals more than humans. It also made creating a found family for myself necessary.

For Rowdy, I was enough and not too much. Me in all my single, messy, heartbroken glory. Unlike humans, dogs didn't stand on societal norms or hierarchies. They just knew to love and accept love in return. The simplicity made them too good for us, but I was thankful nonetheless.

A business clothing store on my right advertised comfortable travel wear. I lingered past the bright open entrance, wondering if I should stop and grab a versatile little black dress in case my luggage got lost in my last-minute travel change snafu. I preferred a more flowy nature vibe than a little black number, but I hadn't thought to put tonight's cocktail party gown in my carry-on before checking my bags. And showing up to the reality show villa in Spain in a limo, looking like I did now, wearing pastel-green lounge sweats from the mall, was not going to happen.

Leather bags and briefcases stood upright on display blocks in the front windows. Mannequins wore sweater vests and collared button-ups with pencil skirts and pressed slacks. None of it called to me, so I picked up my pace. The producers probably had a protocol for wrangling luggage for contestants who missed their flights or had delayed flights. I couldn't be the only one.

I stole another quick peek at my little buddy's image on my phone before tossing it in my purse. Rowdy had nursed me back to the living after the love of my life, my fiancée, broke up with me. He snorted his way into my life about a week after Sonia ended things, and I couldn't have been more grateful to whoever or whatever was watching out for me. He had rooted, played, and slept beside me while I wept, lay despondent, and everything in between. He was magic and deserved all the snuggles and treats in the world.

Unlike my dog, who acted like I could do no wrong, *I* questioned myself for months and months after the breakup. What was wrong with me that Sonia felt she had to end it out of the blue and not allow me to disagree? For how long had she thought about leaving me before doing it? Had she always secretly disliked me, and eventually one day she'd had enough?

To believe I had found my forever person in my partner one moment, only to have that reality smashed to smithereens by said partner the next moment, had a way of seeping toxic doubt into everything.

Who else secretly thought shitty things about me? Who else, when tragedy struck, would blame me for their pain while I worked tirelessly to ease it? In the beginning, it had even affected my job. I found myself scared my clients secretly hated me, somehow knew my most private failings, and judged me for it.

That's when I had to go back to scheduling more appointments with my therapist than the bimonthly maintenance sessions.

My friends had been there for me too, of course, when it happened.

The friends who got the brunt of my confusion-fueled grief were coworkers in the nonprofit I worked for. We spent our weekdays helping children experiencing level-three mental health issues, holding the little hands of strong souls as they learned the harshness of reality too young. It was a reality my own child self related to and my adult self wanted to help others through.

But after months of crying to them about the emotions wrestling inside, I stopped sharing that part of myself. If I was sick of hearing myself, I knew they had to be over it.

Every so often I would realize how long it had been since Sonia and I last talked or saw one another, and a new sense of rejection would roll in like a dense fog to crush the breath out of me. She wasn't going to text or call. She wasn't going to see the social media posts I made public, on my private page, especially for her eyes to scroll across.

My friends didn't know that I secretly hoped she missed me enough to search my socials, see my olive branch posts, and reach out to tell me she was okay. They didn't know about my short stints on dating apps, and how I always deleted them because I kept swiping right on women who reminded me of Sonia—dark fade haircut, casual-cool style, loved dogs, around five foot five, worked in the medical field. It was shallow, immature, and embarrassing. Only Rowdy and I knew how pathetic I could be when it came to her.

I paused from my Sonia thoughts long enough to catch an airport directional sign and turn the last corner. Tall slats of curved bluish glass jutted from shiny white flooring like an ice fortress dropped in the middle of a busy international airport. I slowed to take in the structure as I neared it. A few people's blurred forms moved between the glass rows, as many more hurried around or straight through the thing like it was in their way.

A circular silver plate lay in the floor, at the center of the labyrinth, where a wide walkway separated one side of the glass fortress from the other. Navigating the foot traffic seemed hardly worth the effort to view a plate I'd seen online a couple times over the years. It included the artist's name, Christopher Janney, and a riddle-slash-poem about his vision of the piece.

I tucked into a rounded path with curved glass walls on each side and began my journey. The airport's sounds of chaos hushed to white noise between the thick rows of glass. No longer did distinct people rush by, but colorful blurs moved along and out of my vision. Every few steps, a new random sound or light filled the bubble of space. One step over a metal circle in the floor brought deep blue light streaming up to bounce and reflect. Movement over another circle caused trumpet music to serenade my walk until the next circle revealed what it held.

Using labyrinths as a tool to explain the process of healing to my older clients had proved helpful, which solidified my appreciation of the current walk of intent. There would be no deep reflections found in the overwhelm of an international airport, but I was glad for the short break and the reminder to take time out to center myself during this trip. To always, no matter what, breathe and find my center.

Birdsong and pink light rose from beneath me, and I paused to be in the moment. Had it been Sonia who first told me about this audiovisual art piece in the middle of a Texas airport? I couldn't remember and wondered when she would fade from being so close to the top of my mind all the time. How could someone have such a lasting impact long after they'd disappeared from my life? Her voice whispered on breezes, and her words wove patterns of what could have been, enough to still squeeze the breath from my lungs.

She didn't care about me. It was a fact that took entirely too long to lodge itself in my head and heart. The dark whirlpool of questions surrounding her used to leave me in pieces, trying with everything I didn't have to sew myself together again.

Eventually I decided I was running out of thread. I blocked her number and all her socials the day I called it. I was done waiting for her to miss me enough to reach out. I couldn't wait anymore.

That choice broke me in new ways.

But it also helped me to heal. Keeping the door open for her had held me in limbo, hoping. As long as I fantasized about an eventual happy ending with her, I was keeping myself from experiencing the healing needed to give my own self happiness.

It had been over a year since the heart-in-my-throat, shredded-to-pieces day Sonia shattered my dreams of a future with her. These days, I felt like a new version of myself. A more confident and adventurous version, unafraid to take a chance on love. To take a chance on me.

Not as confident as my friends apparently saw me, though. At our dinner last night, they joked I must have been chosen to be one of the *dramatic* contestants. The show's tension creator.

Of course, I probably shouldn't have told them the part about the casting director's assistant saying, during one of our Zoom meetings, they chose me because they thought I'd shake things up a bit.

I mean, yes, shaking things up had its benefits, but not on television. I preferred to shake up the status quo, people's narrow perceptions. Not shake up hearts.

I had the power to prove them wrong, anyway.

At least that was what I told myself.

I exhaled a cleansing breath, rested my hands on my hips, and tried, yet again, to be in the moment. This trip was about more for me than the remote possibility of meeting someone special. It was my own personal Elly 2.0 release celebration.

I chuckled to myself at my luck. Originally, my layover had been on the East Coast. When I missed my first flight, one of the show's assistants sent over a new itinerary with DFW for my connecting flight. If I hadn't missed my plane, I would have never gotten to experience this artist's offering of contemplative space.

"See," I reminded myself on a whisper, "everything happens for a reason. Including this. Including being late." The synchronicities I had experienced since hearing about the show only solidified my decision to do it. Realizing my reroute included visiting an exhibit I'd wanted to see continued the trend.

Nearing the end of the rounded rows of glass, I decided not to return to the beginning as I remembered the riddle on the main center plate in the sculpture suggested. I took in the strong, curved glass surrounding me as though it was a metaphor for how I intended to show up for myself in the coming weeks of this trip—able to bend, lead with clarity, and stand secure.

The echoed sounds of horse hooves clopping on cobblestone dissipated my inner calm and replaced it with a sense of urgency. A new person had entered the labyrinth behind me.

It was time to move on and move forward. Literally and figuratively.

As I enjoyed my last seconds in the art installation and took a sharp right to exit out the side, I prayed to my higher self, to the universe, to my ancestors and guides and whoever else cared to listen.

Please, don't let this thing I'm about to do be me repeating the same old mistakes of patterns and getting the same old painful consequences.

Please.

And please *make the ghost scent of* her *cologne stop harassing me already.*

Chapter Three

Sonia

When I had mentioned the Dallas Fort Worth airport's glass circle to Elly years ago, I never imagined I would be experiencing it in person on my way to a reality dating show. The thirty-two-foot-wide interactive art installation hadn't passed through my thoughts in years. It never had its own slot on my bucket list. And yet, the moment I realized the show booked my connecting flight through DFW, seeing it became a need of mine.

Each step I took toward *Circling* felt like a step toward Elly, toward a shared moment we discussed but never got to have.

Bright advertisements shifted colors in my peripheral vision from huge mounted screens as the voices of passing travelers grew and shrank in waves. This airport was like all the other big ones, bright, busy, and loud.

The whispered memory of Elly and me talking about visiting this exhibit lingered in my mind like the last bite of a meal I now knew only from recollection. As though for powerfully swift seconds, I could taste the layers of flavor, feel the nourishing comfort and, in those same moments, experience the panic in knowing these will never be my reality again.

Nearing the structure, I caught sight of the circular metal plate in the floor at the center and went right for it. I had watched videos and seen photos of this art piece, sometimes while cuddled up with Elly, with this exact engraved riddle about ending at the beginning always included. Seeing the etching in person made me wish I had brought a piece of plain paper and a crayon to memorialize the moment.

Circling's use of multiple art forms woven together to create one was what first caught my attention when a professor mentioned it in a college class. Back then, I had been more into playing sports than flexing my creativity. So on the rare occasions I felt the need to express myself through art, I dabbled, to experience a little of everything.

I could almost smell and feel Elly again, as I stared at the riddle on the silver plaque on the tiled floor near my Adidas. I stood above the thing, nearly laughing at the serendipity of it all. In more than one way, I was back at the beginning.

Elly had been the first person I mentioned *Circling* to, over burgers after a long week of classes. The conversation had gone the way most went with Elly when I first told her about this exhibit. She came up with ideas for ways to fold it into our dream travel plans. Like, during a connecting flight on our honeymoon.

I gulped to clear my throat. As though I wore shorts and a tank top rather than my blue joggers and hoodie, a chill slunk across my skin.

Forgotten memories teased up by loving thoughts made the worst sneak attacks. They approached positive and happy, seamlessly transitioning to the deep plunge of regret. Strangely, I took comfort in my belief that love and loss went together like sand and paper, able to smooth rough edges or forge weapons.

I had the option to choose for myself whether I would learn and grow from loss or let it wear me down to a prickly asshole. No part of me vibed with being prickly.

Shaking cold tingles from my hands, I pulled my focus from the riddle and kept walking. I rarely believed in signs, and yet I couldn't help but wonder if my strong desire to walk the glass labyrinth was a way of letting Elly go before arriving at the villa in Spain. A way of going back to the beginning to pay homage to my past and start out on a new journey.

My movement activated a speaker beneath me, and I jumped

at the sudden sound of horse hooves trotting. Peering around to see if anyone noticed, I covered my mouth and laughed at myself. We were, after all, in an airport.

One figure left the outer portion of the exhibit in a hurry, but two others lingered in a curved row closer to me, not seeming to be bothered at all. Good.

After going through the exhibit once, to absorb and enjoy, I returned to the beginning to snap pictures and walk through a second time before I made my way to the departure gate.

With what I estimated to be another thirty minutes of wait time before the flight attendants started boarding my East Coast–bound flight, I pulled out the packet Stacy made for me about the bacheloress, Tallia, and settled into a chair across from a floor-to-ceiling window.

Set on relieving my dry throat, I cracked open the seal on my water bottle and took a swig. After another gulp, I screwed the cap back on the cold bottle and flipped through my Tallia packet. The bacheloress was twenty-six, had a master's in social work, and co-ran a nonprofit for underrepresented queer people of color. Impressive. She was born and raised in Massachusetts, graduated from Howard University in Washington, DC, and then returned to her hometown to work for a nonprofit before starting her own with a close friend and colleague.

I turned the page and laughed out loud. Stacy had provided a full-page printout of a screenshot I assumed she captured from Tallia's LinkedIn profile. The producers chose well in their casting of the first bacheloress. Intelligent, educated, compassionate, strong, and beautiful. The next page in the packet featured what I assumed were copied and pasted images from Tallia's social media pages. In some, she wore gowns and a full face of makeup, her black hair in braids or updos. In other photos she wore suits, minimal makeup, and her hair slicked back tightly to her skull. Whichever her look, each photo showed the sparkle of vitality and joy in her eyes, the hint of confidence in her smirks and smiles.

She had the rare ability to wear the aesthetics of femme and masc with equal success. She was successful and in a caring field of work. Hell, even her teeth were perfect. And yet all I felt shifting inside was the possibility of needing to hit the restroom before my flight boarded. No way the water hit me that quickly. I was just antsy. I had hoped, by now, the idea of meeting Tallia on the other side of this flight would have the power to rustle up excitement for new love. Sitting at my gate, minutes away from boarding, the lack of such feelings became an uncomfortable reality.

Airplanes taxied the runway. An elderly couple in my row of chairs joked about a last-minute restroom visit. Departure-change announcements crackled over the loudspeaker. Passengers were called to their gate's desk. All the distractions seemed more interesting than my reading material. I doubted I'd feel different when I arrived in Spain and worried this trip would be one huge mistake that revealed itself over and over.

I had gone through *Circling* for a second time hoping to feel a sense of new beginning, a fresh start before boarding for a big trip. As though the first was the wash cycle, I tried again, hoping the Elly-aches would come out in the rinse. No such luck.

Not that I believed luck had anything to do with it. No, what I felt had more to do with grief than luck or anything else. Over the last year, I had gotten to know mourning a little too well. So much so, I often found myself wondering if melancholy was going to become a part of my personality now. If too much loss in a small amount of time had a way of changing a person permanently, like a bone broken in too many places at once. Some fractures were inoperable, unfixable, leaving the bone forever weakened, prone to future breaks.

Within minutes of loading my luggage cart at the Madrid-Barajas Airport's baggage area, I spotted my driver, a man in a black button-up and matching slacks. He held a sign with my name printed in bold above the show's branding, a bundle of violets.

"Nice to meet you," I said, offering him a handshake when he reached to take my cart of bags.

He smiled, shook my hand, and beelined for my luggage. He led us through a skybridge to a multilevel parking garage. A wall of hot, humid night air greeted us as we exited the enclosed bridge and stepped into the brightly lit parking garage. He barreled the luggage cart, piled with my three black suitcases, toward a hall of elevators. I jogged to keep up.

Cool air blew into the small elevator space as soon as the doors shut. Relief washed over me. Maybe wearing joggers and a hoodie for comfort wasn't the best idea when traveling to Spain in the summer. I pulled the hoodie over my head and hung it over my arm. Using the reflection in the silver elevator walls, I smoothed the clump of hair sticking out directly above my fade.

My hair's texture represented what I thought was a unique combination of hereditary genetics—my dad's Latin and Germanic, and my mom's Irish and Korean—that resulted in thick, dark brown tresses that couldn't hold a curl and also had a thing for sticking straight out if not cut just perfectly.

"Am I the only one you're picking up?" I asked the man's reflection after fixing mine. He wore his black shoulder-length hair in a ponytail. A joke comparing his hair to mine knit together in my mind but never made it past my lips.

My hair was too unruly to grow out long enough for a ponytail. I only knew it couldn't hold a curl because the last time it was long enough to style, I had been a junior high student with barely wavy elbow-length hair at her last middle school dance. The next dance I attended had been during my freshman year of high school, sporting a new fade and a new look.

He caught my eyes in the elevator wall reflection. When the doors dinged and opened, he navigated my luggage cart out of the boxlike space and into the expanse of the parking garage.

"You're the only one," he said, staring forward as we passed black car after black car. It seemed we were in a type of business parking level.

I liked to think I could make friendly conversation with anyone, and I wasn't going to let jet lag ruin that for me. "How was your day?" I asked, keeping his pace in stride beside him.

He stopped at a black sedan. I only made it one car farther before I realized and doubled back.

"Should I help?" I asked, as the man heaved my suitcases into the trunk. It felt weird to watch and do nothing.

"I got it," was all he said, until he finished loading the bags, shut the trunk, and opened my door.

"Oh, I could have gotten that," I said, feeling awkward with nothing to do.

He closed my door, slid into the driver's seat, and started the ignition.

My neck probably looked like it was attached to a bobblehead once he pulled the sedan away from the airport and onto city streets. Old Europe architecture melded with twenty-first century technology as lit signs hung in windows and on the tops of buildings. Cobblestone streets lined with trees old enough to have witnessed countless generations of life existed alongside people talking on their cell phones.

On an average night at work, I met maybe twenty people, most on one of the worst days of their lives. Helping them to feel a little more human and less of a number was one of the newer goals I'd picked up from Dad's time in the hospital. It naturally extended to out-of-work interactions, so sitting silently in the back seat made me uncomfortable.

"My name's Sonia Comstock, what's yours?" I asked more directly, leaning forward toward the center console.

A smile flickered across his lips while he watched the road. "Tony Chavez. Nice to meet you, Sonia."

Happy to know the name of the other person in the car with me, I leaned into the comfortable seat. "Tony, are you driving for the show throughout filming?"

"I am," he said with a nod.

"Sounds like an interesting gig," I offered.

Tony gave a laugh. "You have no idea. It's just day one, and it's already getting crazy."

We left the cobblestone streets for a highway, wide and nearly empty. Properties speckled the purple hills in the distance with flickering lights. The sun's last stretches splashed like fire along the horizon. Pop music, turned down in volume to a mumble of rhythm, added a relaxing lull.

"Crazy, huh?" I asked. Exhaustion covered me like a weighted blanket. I let my eyes close while I spoke. "As in people didn't show, or early gameplay?"

Tony blew a sharp exhale. "As in, we clocked in to pick up contestants and take them to the villa as they arrived today. And we found out that's not what's happening. A whole surprise twist thing."

I opened my eyes and leaned forward. Nobody liked last-minute changes to international travel plans. "What's happening?" I asked, my relaxation dissipated. "We're going to the villa, right?"

"No," Tony answered. "You're in group B."

"Group B?" I asked, trying not to let panic seep in. "Where's group B staying?"

Tony shook his head. "A completely separate house, not the villa."

CHAPTER FOUR

Elly

"Welcome! Welcome to the violet ceremony room," a silver-haired woman in black slacks and button-up said to the crowd of sapphic contestants I walked into the small room with. Small in comparison to the villa's living room and kitchen, where we had all been moments earlier.

Like a herd of pack animals, we shuffled into the dimly lit room. Another staff member—they all wore black clothing and earpieces—directed those of us leading the group toward a three-tiered metal platform that reminded me of my short-lived choir days in school.

As seemed to be my trend for the evening, I strategized how to get where I needed to go, despite the flowy floor-length gown I wore. After catching my shoe's heel on the forest-green tulle while stepping from the limo to meet Tallia in front of the villa, and nearly making a fool of myself on television, I had hoped the worst was behind me.

Contestants moved around me to follow directions and make their way to the top of the stand. Grabbing a handful of tulle, I stood beside the lowest tier of the platform and lifted my leg up and over it. Before I could plant it firmly on the other side, a contestant pushed past me and I lost what little balance I had.

I released the tulle and shoved my hand out toward the platform to break my fall.

"Oh, got you," someone said, laughing as they grabbed my elbow with fingers tipped in deep pink acrylics and righted me.

Utter embarrassment froze me in place. The tall woman shimmied as she fixed the hem of her hot pink miniskirt dress. She arched a perfect brow and leaned in. "I say we stay here on the bottom tier and let the mascs in slacks and flats climb the higher tiers of terror."

"I vote yes," I answered. "Thank you."

She helped me stand upright before I held my hand out for her to join. Contestants made their way around us and past us as the room filled.

"My name is Sapphire," she said, reaching a hand to shake mine. "She her."

"Good to meet you," I responded. "And again, thank you for saving me."

She smiled, displaying perfect white teeth. "Anytime." Sapphire's light hair shifted in wavy curls down her shoulders and back as she turned her torso to look the room over. "This is weird, isn't it?"

"Incredibly," I answered without looking at her. "What happened to the cocktail party?" Now that I found my spot, the room's decorations and commotion held my visual focus.

Show staff began ushering contestants to stand beside the platform and in front of it, reminding them to squeeze in. Lavender and lilacs cascaded from iron-looking wall sconces attached to deep purple walls. White candles in varying sizes grouped together on the floor in the corners of the room and the centers of small tabletops along the walls. The candle color and flames popped as a light contrast to the dark ambience.

After meeting Tallia, who seemed delightful and overwhelmed, I had been directed to enter the villa and join the waiting contestants. Tallia entered the villa about a half hour after me and couldn't have had more than twenty minutes to get to know the contestants before show staff introduced us to the...

"She called it the violet ceremony room," I said to Sapphire the moment it clicked. In the emails, the show's promotional image was a bundle of violets illustrated to look like flowers from a vintage seed catalog. At the time, I had thought it was a cute play on the Sappho theme. Now I realized it represented more than Sappho.

Sapphire's blue eyes widened. "You're right." She scanned the room and caught my gaze again. "I think we're going into our first elimination round."

I thought so too, but it made no sense. "How is she supposed to know who to kick off this soon?"

Sapphire shook her head. "And why do they have this little stand when only a third of the contestants can actually fit on it?"

If I thought the room was crowded with contestants, moments after our crowd found their spots, show staff carrying video recorders and fuzzy boom mics filled what was left of the space, lining the walls across from us.

"Is this the elimination already?" someone asked the incoming show staff.

"I haven't even had a chance to talk with Tallia," another complained.

Random questions shot from contestants to show staff but fell on unreceptive ears. Still, contestants continued to ask while staff set up their cameras and seemed to only listen to their earpieces.

"Hello, Sapphics!" I heard the joy in his voice before I saw his smiling face. "My name is Kamal, he him, and I'm your host for this pilot season of *The Sapphic Bacheloress!*"

The only man not dressed in all black, Kamal made his way to the center of the room, sporting pressed maroon slacks, light brown leather loafers, and a silver V-neck top that sparkled in the candlelight. His black hair appeared to be expertly cut with sharp lines and a fade mascs would kill for.

Two staff members bustled around him, securing a mic to his shirt and adding powder to his forehead. When they finished and fled the room, he cleared his throat and flashed us a smile. "We're about to begin filming, but I wanted to first introduce myself and prepare you while they finish setting up."

As we shared a collective sigh, I felt my shoulders drop. Sapphire nudged my bare arm with hers. I liked this new friend of mine and intended to make her just that, my friend.

"While I do not claim to be sapphic"—Kamal paused to let a few contestants snicker—"I am an LGBTQ family member and proud to be the host of such an ingenious concept. Because, really, if we're going to show down-to-earth people with pure hearts who are willing to grow for love, we're going to be showing sapphics."

Our group cheered, me included.

Kamal looked to the silver-haired woman who first directed us into the room. She gave a nod and his smile grew bigger. Red indicator lights on the filming devices around the room turned on. Everyone quieted. Our host stared into the camera nearest the crowd at the base of the platform, pointed at him and the center of the room.

"Hello, and welcome to *The Sapphic Bacheloress*'s first elimination, the violet ceremony," Kamal started. He raised his arms motioning to the walls behind and beside him. "Is it not decadent and oozing with sapphic intimacy?"

Contestants chuckled and agreed.

"I don't know," Kamal said, pretending to scratch the sharply edged hairline on his temple in thought. "Maybe we should ask the Sapphic Bacheloress herself what she thinks. Oh, Tallia?"

The double doors separating this room from the rest of the villa swung open, and the contestants on the floor, nearest the doors, gasped with excitement. Seconds later, Tallia strode past our platform full of people and stopped less than an arm's length from Kamal.

The bacheloress wore a black fitted maxi dress with a high neckline and open back. Rhinestone braids wove together from the back of her neck, across the top of her right shoulder, and down her dress like a sparkling snake twisting itself across her chest. She wore her black hair slicked back at the base of her skull, with rhinestone snake earrings to match her dress.

"It's all so gorgeous!" she exclaimed, slowly turning to take in the room. "It even smells like lavender and violets in here."

"Do the sights and scents help at all with the sting of elimination nipping at your heels?" Kamal asked, his head tilted.

Tallia groaned. "No, but we might as well get it over with."

As though on cue, Kamal ushered the bacheloress to a table against the wall littered with candles and a silver covered platter. He grazed his fingers along the silver dome's handle. "Before I lift this lid," he said, in a warning voice, "I feel like I need to preface with an explanation."

Tallia took a wary step backward.

"I'm sure you've noticed the large number of contestants," Kamal said.

Tallia gave a slow nod. Candlelight reflected from her dress, sparkling deep oranges and reds across her chest each time she moved.

"*The Sapphic Bacheloress* is more than a reality dating show," Kamal said, removing his hand from the dome's handle to motion to the contestants. "It's a sapphic human experience experiment." When Tallia didn't respond, he continued, "You already know those eliminated after tonight get to spend the rest of filming at a wellness center. But what you don't know is the wellness center is just *one* of the growth opportunities we have planned for you all."

"And what's on that platter is another?" Tallia asked, her hand on her hip.

Kamal lifted the silver dome and set it beside the platter on the table. A line of purple bundles lay atop one another. Violets. "Tonight, based only on first impressions, you will eliminate over half the people here today."

Tension filled the room. Contestants looked to one another. Sapphire nudged my arm with hers.

Seriously? This was their big growth reveal? That most of us were going home?

"There's only eight bundles, though," Tallia said, concern leaking through her voice. "And more than twenty people."

Heat filled my cheeks. My favorite part of the dress I wore, the lace and sequined applique, now felt like a chest binder, restricting me from taking a deep breath. I kept my blondish-brown topknot in place with a forest-green pin, while the bottom portion of my hair poured down my back. The idea had been to show off my shaved sides and the length of my hair. But with the room full of bodies, all growing more nervous by the second, it felt as though my temperature rose. A bead of sweat collected at my hairline and wound down my freshly shaved lotus undercut.

I came all this way, took time off work, arranged multiple weeks' worth of house and dog watching, and got my hopes up for what? To be sent back home within a day of my arrival?

"The show's gonna be over before it starts," I whispered to myself.

Sapphire grabbed my hand and held it. Her support gifted me a wave of confidence. I squeezed her palm to signal *thank you*.

"Eight bundles of violets for the eight sapphics here tonight you wish to take with you on the journey ahead." Kamal responded to Tallia's concern over the number of flower bundles. "Whose first impression blew you away? Who did you have instant chemistry with? Who have you not gotten a chance to get a feel for, but they intrigue you just the same?"

Tallia slowly scanned the contestants crowding the room and piled on the three-tiered platform. She inhaled and released a breath. "Okay," she said, reaching for a bundle of violets from the silver platter on the table beside her.

"One last thing," Kamal quipped, "that may matter. Or it may not."

Tallia shook her head, and I thought I saw her roll her eyes.

Kamal's expression softened. He gave a nod and sighed. "I know, not knowing is the worst," he said. "But it also limits expectations and opens our minds to new possibilities. So know this, tomorrow this contest will take a twisty turn into a territory synonymous with sapphic. You will soon find out which contestants are flexible, able to roll with the punches. And which are still *hung up*."

The bacheloress clutched the stems of the violets and held the bundle to her chest. She closed her eyes, exhaled, opened her eyes, and began to speak. "First, I want to thank each and every one of you for putting yourself out there, for flying all the way to Spain to meet me. I'm sorry I didn't have more time to know you all, and I'm sorry I have to do this based purely on the superficial."

If Tallia's statement offended Kamal, he didn't show it. "Whenever you're ready," he said.

Tallia gave a nod. "I am."

❖

Nursing a subtle hangover from the villa's violet ceremony followed by a stress-fueled cocktail party, I wiped my index finger under each eye to clean smudges from last night's makeup. I tossed the used wet wipe into the wastebasket beside the dresser, put my rainbow-framed glasses back on, and leaned in to examine my reflection.

Behind me, my room shone in a bright cheerfulness I wasn't feeling. Morning sunlight streamed in from a glass balcony door and spilled across the floral comforter crumpled into a mound in the center of the four-poster bed. My room looked like the set of a period piece movie, if I ignored the lamp and digital clock on the side table.

My bamboo shower caddy called to me from my peripheral vision. It sat at the edge of the dresser, waiting. A fresh wash to start the day sounded perfect. But first, caffeine.

After a dramatic night, I hoped we would be able to get a moment to catch our breath today. The bags under my eyes begged for a nap.

Last night's opening violet ceremony hit me with stark new perspectives on my favorite dating show contestants. They too had to stand alone, in a crowd, on display, waiting to be chosen by a near-stranger. I didn't look forward to the next ceremony. It made no sense how being deemed worthy by someone we just met could matter so much, but it did.

The bacheloress started the elimination with a packed room.

By the time the eliminated contestants were ushered into waiting passenger vans and we survivors were sharing a toast with flutes of champagne, our group changed dramatically in size. We went from a packed room to eight contestants.

A short, clear knock captured my attention. With a huff, I removed myself from my reflection and headed for the dark bedroom door. Before I closed the distance, a folded paper slipped under the door and slid across the wooden floor into the ball of my foot.

"What do we have here?" I asked nobody in particular as I picked it up and ran my hand over what felt like thick cardstock with tattered edges, made to replicate antique paper.

I'd rewatched all the reality dating shows I could find before coming on this one, to know what to expect and begin mentally preparing to pivot throughout the curveballs thrown. In reality TV, curveballs were *always* thrown.

But no amount of show-binging could have prepared me for the emotional dichotomy of adventure and vulnerability, when the foundation of expectations cracked, leaving room for new unknowns to sprout. Saying good-bye to more than half the contestants I met last night threw me. Elimination-style dating shows tended to maintain a large group of contestants for more than a couple of hours. And decorative cards sealed with melted wax tended to be date announcements.

Except this wasn't a note inside a basket of goodies left on the kitchen table or delivered to whoever answered the front door. And it was too early in the game for the cardstock message to be a group date announcement.

I thought back to my many hours of research alongside my trusty assistant, Rowdy. I supposed with the small number of contestants left, date cards were a slight possibility. The idea, though, felt like too much too soon. I knew I was here to date, but I needed time to catch my breath. Dating back home, in familiar territory, had been a short-lived failure. I wasn't in a hurry to dip back in the moment I touched ground. Once I got familiar with my new surroundings, I would start to feel more confident and flirtatious. I hoped.

The purple wax seal snapped with a bend, allowing me to unfold the paper and read the calligraphy out loud.

Congratulations on your first full day in Casa del Amor. In an hour, brunch will be served in the courtyard, along with exciting news. Brace yourself for the fresh look of old faces, and the opportunity for a love of a lifetime.

I placed the open note card on the dresser and paced the room, from the far edge of the dresser to the balcony door and back. Moving helped me to think.

The fresh look of old faces. I couldn't image what that meant. Makeovers?

An hour. I paused to stare at myself in the mirror atop the clawfoot dresser. My plan to caffeinate before all else was ruined. I didn't have time to shower, either. With less than an hour to fix last night's mess of makeup and hair product, I considered my list of priorities.

I grabbed another wet wipe from the package in my shower caddy and went to work on my eyebrows and the rest of my face. With my cheeks naked as the day I was born, and probably just as red, I flashed a smile at the mirror.

"Don't forget to brush your teeth," I told myself as I grabbed for the plain black hair clip attached to the shower caddy.

I piled my hair on the crown of my head, simultaneously exposing my lotus flower undercut and hiding last night's hair product. Today's style had more to do with convenience than appearance. Considering the fact brought a twinge of insecurity.

Normally, I took the personal opinions of others as their perceptions based on their experiences and none of my business. But this experience blurred that line in a way I was still trying to wrap my mind around.

One day here and I'm already in my head.

I reminded myself of the science behind what I was experiencing. New, unfamiliar territory coupled with matters of the heart, which had a way of nicking misunderstood childhood hurts. It was classic, textbook behavioral health, and totally something I had in me to learn from and overcome.

With toothpaste and a toothbrush in hand, I padded down the hall to the shared bathroom. We were probably going to be surprised with brunch, mimosas, facials, and massages with Tallia, after last night's brutal elimination. I needed to stop assuming the worst.

CHAPTER FIVE

Sonia

Four of us sat in soft brown leather bucket seats in an SUV, headed for *The Sapphic Bacheloress*'s villa. Colognes and perfumes mixed in the air-conditioned vehicle, along with stiff laughter and anxiety-filled comments. Except for LeeAnn. I wasn't sure if she had an anxious bone in her lanky body.

"They're gonna be so happy to see us," LeeAnn said, after Katy asked for feedback on her red lipstick. "I'm glad we're the ones who get to go." She wore her blondish-brown hair in a ponytail at the nape of her neck, with a light blue polo and beige fitted ankle pants.

"You're not worried about the twist?" Toren asked. They sat in my back row and reminded me of someone I would see pushing a book cart in a library, in their maroon vest, coffee-colored slacks, and brown loafers with actual pennies in the exposed part of the shoes' tongues. An outstretched crow tattoo covered their exposed chest, the tips of its wings hiding under their vest.

"It won't be anything we can't handle," LeeAnn assured us like she knew.

Last night had been the show's first violet ceremony, and this morning we were heading to our first day of filming. None of us had known we were the backup contestants, group B, as Tony so skillfully hinted. Unfortunately, his hint didn't register until Elise, one of the show's producers, sat us down in the living room of the rental house we stayed at and explained that some of us would not get the chance to see the villa.

My chat with Tony at least prepared me, partially. I planned to thank him if I saw him again.

This morning, four of us piled into the car we now rode in, and the other three housemates got into a similar SUV that Tony drove. They left for the airport, and we were on our way to twist shit up at the villa.

I wondered who else stayed up last night and considered calling it quits and heading home with the airport-bound, after hearing the news. Normally, a vent text to Stacy or my mom would help, but they dropped the bombshell after we turned our phones in.

"Do you think I went over the top for a brunch, though?" Katy asked, rocking her rainbow platforms on the black rubber mat in front of her seat.

"You're going to blow them away," I said and meant it. "Are you kidding? I mean, look at you." I waved a newly manicured hand toward her. Never one for polish, my nails were trimmed short, filed down smooth, and clean.

"Anyone else learn about Tallia while waiting?" Toren asked. They adjusted their dark-framed glasses.

I considered mentioning a few things I'd gleaned from the packet Stacy gathered for me but decided against it out of self-preservation. Having to watch some of our group be sent home before getting the opportunity to begin was a punch to the gut I didn't see coming. What little trust I had for this reality dating arrangement hinged solely on the adventure of it all, and blindsiding people didn't feel adventurous. It felt tacky and manipulative, not anything I wanted to be a part of.

"Like, are you talking about stalking Tallia?" LeeAnn asked Toren with a teasing laugh.

I caught Toren's eye roll response and smiled. I related.

"No," Toren answered, straightening their suit vest. "Research. Learning about the person you're trying to woo to know they're right for you, and to assure them that who they are matters. Because you're not dating a placeholder, you're dating a human. Accepting and respecting their autonomy as their own person and not just the person who'll make you feel good till they don't."

Toren and LeeAnn were discussing the same topic, dating, but on two distinct levels. I wondered if the contestants at the villa were more like LeeAnn or Toren. One I could handle for a few weeks. The other, not so much.

LeeAnn shrugged. "Never needed it before."

Toren lifted a dark eyebrow. "Never needed to *make an effort*?"

"Speaking of not needing it," LeeAnn added, "how long have you all been single?"

"Six months," Katy answered.

"Almost a year," Toren said. "Why does that matter?"

"None of your business," I answered on the heels of Toren's comment. Because it didn't matter.

LeeAnn chose to ignore my response and honed in on Toren's. "See," LeeAnn explained, "it's been a month for me. Not even. And before that, a few weeks, and before that, maybe a month. Never needed research as a crutch." She placed her hands, palm down, on her lap as though she'd given the last arguments of a winning case.

"I don't know that that's proof to support your point," Toren countered. Her soft jab went over LeeAnn's head as we exited a public road and turned on to a long, tree-lined cobblestone driveway. A huge set of wrought-iron gates sat open, allowing the car access to continue up a hill dotted with manicured trees and grass.

Shifting in my seat for a better view, I looked out the windshield. Thousands of old stones, set into place like a red carpet, led us up a hill to the main event. Terra-cotta roof tiles caught my attention first, with the rest of the three-story villa exposing itself as the SUV crested the hill it sat upon. Our vehicle entered the circular driveway and pulled past the stone steps leading to the building. Arched windows and wrought-iron balconies dotted the sprawling yellowish-beige stucco building, emphasizing the arched entrance.

The vehicle slowed to a stop at the farthest side of the villa's looped driveway. Our driver said nothing, but Elise and a few other show staff came out a gate beside the villa to greet us.

Piling out of the car, each of us stretched and quietly took in the expanse of our current situation. Late morning sun rays rested lazily upon a fountain at the center of the circular drive where little, round colorful birds bathed and chirped in the bubbling water. The absence of traffic noise and the inclusion of birdsong calmed my racing heart just enough to pretend I felt cool as a cucumber.

"Welcome!" Elise whispered loudly, her arms in the air, one hand still clinging to her phone. Two staff members flanked her, both dressed in black pants and button-ups, one holding a clipboard and the other an iPad.

I wondered when they would tell us why last night's housemates went home this morning—why they were chosen and not us. And why none of us mentioned it on our way here.

LeeAnn broke off from the pack to stand in front of the villa's stone steps leading up to what I assumed was the front entrance—huge, engraved wooden double doors, lined with ornately twisted wrought iron. With hands on her hips, she began climbing the steps.

Elise called out in a harsh whisper, loud enough to be heard, "No, LeeAnn, not that way."

Our producer made a *gather-round* motion and we silently obeyed. "Okay," she started a little too quietly to hear over the fountain's bubbling and birds splashing.

We took a step or two in, like football players coming in for the pregame huddle. In a way it felt like it too.

Katy spoke up. "So, if we're not going in…"

Elise placed her index finger in front of her lips to shush Katy. "Sorry," Elise quickly followed up, "they're filming on the side garden patio, a post–violet ceremony brunch to welcome their newest contestants."

She flashed a smile that quickly dissipated as her gaze focused past us. She pressed the black earbud into her ear. "They're almost ready for you," she said without looking at us.

Elise ushered us to the left of the villa, show staff still flanking her as we followed, single file. A wooden gate swung open, revealing a narrow walkway of stones that wound through sections of a garden where lavender and sage bushes lived, with trees of varying sizes, shapes, and shades of green offering shade to plants and curved cement benches.

More staff members stood inside the gate, waiting for us. They were dressed similarly to the two near Elise, but they wore white aprons and held silver platters of what looked like lavender-colored cocktails in flute glasses, each decorated with a delicate violet, its stem secured within crushed ice.

The contestants I could now hear but not see let free a burst of group laughter. My heart rate amped to a new quickness.

"Okay, it's almost time," Elise warned us. The staff person holding the iPad made their way to her side and showed her the screen.

"Thanks," she told them before they took a few steps back and out of her way.

"Sonia?"

I perked up. "Yeah?"

"You'll carry the tray with the most glasses on it," she instructed, before rattling off which platters belonged to which of us.

The staff member carrying my platter positioned it securely in my grasp and turned to disappear down the stone path and into the villa through a side door. I held mine securely with a hand on each side. Not dropping a tray of five full glasses in front of a bunch of strangers while being filmed for television mattered more to me than looking cool.

LeeAnn rested her platter on the palm of one hand, with three flutes stationed at the center. Her cocky smile pointed at Toren for some reason.

Once the four of us lined up, each with our silver tray of drinks, Elise stood between us and the bend in the stone path leaving the side garden area for the back of the villa. I wondered how many acres comprised this villa, and how many little secret gardens it hid.

"It's almost time," Elise said, her tone rising with excitement. "There are a few things you all need to be aware of before we head in. First, make sure you go to the table with the chairs that correspond to the number of glasses you carry." She tilted her head toward LeeAnn in front of Katy who stood in front of Toren. I didn't mind being at the back of the line. "For instance, you've got three glasses, so you'll go to the table with three chairs total, including your own."

The producer's face softened as she surveyed the four of us with a smile. "We wanted to make this show unique, special, different."

"Healing," Toren added.

"Exactly," Elise confirmed.

"Sapphic," LeeAnn included.

Elise gave a nod. "Sapphic and healing, yes. In the real sapphic dating world, seeing your ex connected to your friend groups is a normal thing and something you have to navigate. Sometimes, it shows you how much you're meant to be together. Other times, it shows you the opposite. Either way, it can be confirming and edifying, aiding your self-growth and understanding."

Her spiel sounded like she was reading from a note card. The whole thing set my nerves on a new level of edge.

"You four are the exes of some of the contestants left after last night's violet ceremony," Elise explained. "Tallia does not know whose ex you are. None of the contestants know. If you're truly healed and ready for a relationship, your ex and you will show this by maturely navigating dating others. If you're not ready, well, that'll be obvious too."

My stomach dropped to my Adidas.

Outside of my turbulent high school romantic life, I had one ex. Just imagining her sitting on the other side of the stone path I stood upon forced me to fight back hot stinging tears. I should have listened to my gut and left this morning with the others headed to the airport.

I came here to celebrate my dad's memory and my own journey of grief and letting go. I flew to Spain to get acquainted with the new me—a more defined and clarified version after the storm of loss washed away the debris of misaligned pride and fear.

I came for a vacation, not an excruciating walk down memory lane to see the sights I would never get to touch again.

Forcing myself to keep steady and show no emotional tells, two feelings warred within my perfectly still body: the deep desire to turn around and leave, and the absolute need to run to her.

My Elly.

Chapter Six

Elly

Our host, Kamal, stood in the center of the cobblestone courtyard. Water bubbled up from the circular center of a granite fountain behind him. Greenery flourished in every direction, standing tall in bushes, winding up beams, climbing down huge clay pots and around statues.

This spot of the property felt a few degrees cooler than the rest and definitely lighter and more aromatic. As if someone had taken a café and plopped it in the center of an antique mansion's courtyard.

Kamal fit in, in his deep pink slacks, black V-neck, and dark brown loafers, sans socks. So did Sapphire, who sat beside me at our wrought-iron table, looking so European in her flowy light pink summer dress and floppy barely pink sun hat. Her long blond hair spilled out from beneath the hat and down her exposed back.

I, on the other hand, matched our host, in my baby-blue capris, white V-neck, and strappy brown sandals. When I first saw Kamal's outfit, the similarities didn't bother me. Now, though, my anticipation morphed to anxiety. None of the new staff on the patio had exited the villa with carts full of facial or makeover supplies. There were no trays of little sandwiches or bite-size cakes.

Where was the food?

"Rolling," a cameraperson announced.

I fought the urge to find the voice and focused on our host, about to reveal the tantalizing next steps to this process, according to the note slid under my door.

Our bunch had been whittled pretty intensely. I took stock as I surveyed the patio for hints of what the note card alluded to. If most of the other seven remaining contestants had slept in like I had, they too were longing for caffeine and likely breakfast to soak up last night's libations. It wasn't hard to imagine why most of us were on edge.

Tallia walked out through the glass patio door from the villa, with two producers close behind. A long yellow skirt hugged her hips and spilled down her legs. Her high-necked black crop top highlighted her figure and fit abs. She made a sundress outfit look edgy, and I was here for it. The world needed more edgy women.

I turned away from Tallia to smile at Sapphire, who didn't seem to notice me. My new friend's winged, black-lined eyes opened wide as they took in the bacheloress.

Tallia found her spot beside Kamal in front of the fountain as the contestants quieted. She wore her hair up, with cornrows in front and the box braids in back pulled up into a clip, their ends sticking out like a crown around her head. She reminded me of a goddess in gold.

"Wonder why there's extra chairs?" Kamal asked with an impish grin. He gestured toward Tallia's assigned table closest to the fountain, which sat five, with one chair open.

The patio stilled, all eyes on the host and his big reveal. Water bubbled and splashed in the fountain. Birds sang and conversed from nearby branches and perched at the edges of the fountain's basin.

I peered toward where Tallia had exited the villa to see if anyone waited inside, for their grand entrance on to the show. But the scene on the other side of the glass looked dark, empty and still.

"Well?" Tallia gave in. She looked around the patio. "Now you're making me nervous!"

I counted each of the empty chairs. Four.

Kamal lifted his gaze to include the contestants in the

conversation. "What do we think, all? Does this upsetting chair situation call for lavender mimosas?"

Laughter, clapping, and agreement poured toward Kamal from the contestants, as though he'd pulled a fast one and it had all been a joke. A gate at one side of the villa separating us from what looked like another type of garden on the side yard area opened. Kamal stretched his arm out for Tallia to focus on the side of the villa. A line of impeccably dressed people walked through the gate, single-file.

Only, these were not waiters or the show staff. The way they were lined up, I could only see the first person's face. But they weren't wearing the regular all black and a button-up.

This group was colorful. And queer.

I always loved the array of looks and vibes found in a queer crowd. Our styles deviated from mainstream in the best of ways, if you asked me. Shaved heads, long curly hair, buzzcuts and fades, matched with Converse, Vans, Doc Martens, and heels.

"Oh," Sapphire squeaked.

"New contestants," I whispered, assuming that meant more awful eliminations to whittle the group back down.

Along with my fellow contestants, I eyed the line of new people entering the courtyard. As the line came closer, the person wearing rainbow heels broke out to walk toward the other small table. In front of them was a tall, lean androgynous person with blondish-brown hair, wearing beige fitted pants and a light blue top. They headed to our table with their tray of three purple mimosas.

The face of the next in line came to view, a plainly dressed person with a pin secured to their vest that looked like a they/them pin. I couldn't read that far. They veered toward the same table where the woman in rainbow heels now sat.

My focus bounced to the person walking behind them. The last newest contestant was trying to look confident traversing cobblestones, holding a silver tray of cocktails. I did not envy them.

Crisp black and white classic Adidas navigated the bumpy ground with ease, sneaker laces barely peeking out from under the hem of their beige cargos. My gaze trailed north to a black, short-sleeve polo, the fabric barely showing ribbed vertical lines, thanks to the sunlight. I smiled at the words tattooed across her arms as she expertly carried five mimosas on a tray.

Wait.

My smile dropped before my brain caught up.

I knew those quotes. Against my inner insistence, I looked up to confirm.

Like words unsaid and tears not shed, a guttural cry I didn't realize I carried cracked through its fragile casing and climbed up my throat to expose itself to the woman who created it. I clamped my mouth shut too late, and what sounded like a painful yelp made its way out.

My less than quiet response caught her attention. Her dark eyes locked on mine.

Raw, burning anger suddenly bloomed up my core, like a mushrooming atomic bomb, shaking my limbs as I worked to contain its growing power. The unrequited love I was forced to bury because of her rose from its grave like a zombie set on devouring what was left of my heart.

She nearly tripped over a cobblestone.

I automatically leaned forward, as if to prepare to jump from my seat and catch her, to save her.

The words pulsed through every limb, every muscle, and clung to every inhale.

It's her. It's her.

It's my Sonia!

Like nothing more than a spectator, I watched as the person wearing the blue polo placed their tray of glasses on our table and asked both Sapphire and me if they could join us.

I only stared at Sonia as she righted herself, broke our eye contact, and made her way to Tallia's table. My ex was already smiling and laughing with our bacheloress, whose goddess eyes seemed to light up for her.

Tallia urged Sonia to have a seat.

My throat felt sandpaper dry.

Any confidence I had in my personality, in my appearance, in my right to be on this show slinked off into the shadows. Sonia had a special ability to find the one string to pull to unravel me in seconds. Without even trying.

Sonia was charismatic and personable. Tallia would melt from her compliments, feel seen, and fall for her. I wished I had never given her the map to my heart, the knowledge of my inner worlds. Enough for her to trample everything I held dear.

The magic of feeling seen by Sonia was like being filled with the warmest, most comforting liquid. The kind that oozed into your sores and cracks and bound you back together again.

She looked different than when we were together. I hadn't seen her in person since it all happened a year ago. She walked taller, looked stronger somehow. And she was still just as gorgeous as always.

No! No thinking about her.

"Please know…" Kamal said, jolting me from my thoughts as though he'd yelled my name.

The crowd quieted from the uproar of excitement and chatter. I stared at our host as he went on about something to do with healing from past connections, and choosing between the past and the future, and knowing the difference. Despite my efforts to understand why Sonia was here, I couldn't make sense of Kamal's explanation.

All I saw was her, even when my eyes were closed.

Cameras panned away from Kamal and settled on the tables, abuzz with hushed chatter and tense laughter. Kamal's smile dropped and he exited the courtyard through a side gate with a handful of show staff following behind.

My distractions abandoned me.

"Can you tell I'm shaking?" I asked Sapphire and immediately regretted it.

When she didn't answer, I risked a look at her face.

She wasn't scrutinizing my sudden behavior change, or confused at my shaking arms and bouncing leg. She and the new woman were already talking best- and worst-case show twist scenarios.

They sipped their mimosas. I grabbed the last one on the tray and gulped down half the contents to wet my throat.

As I absently moved the violet stem out of my way to finish my drink, I plotted my pivot. No one would be able to stop me from walking out, right?

But then what? I wasn't home. I was stuck in a foreign country. *Ugh.*

"Hey, Elly, you okay?" Sapphire reached out to me across the table. I reached back and gripped her hand for a quick reassuring squeeze.

Had Kamal mentioned revealing whose ex belonged to whom? The thought of announcing to the world how Sonia rejected and discarded me with ease made my stomach turn and my eyes fill with tears.

It took all the self-control I had to sit in my chair and not bolt for the gate to get away from the one woman I would have done absolutely anything for.

The one who couldn't love me back the same.

How dared she? How dared Sonia show up here and make everything confusing and harder and sad. I had to push through. I could cry soon.

I imagined a shell growing around me, protecting my emotions from leaking out. I inhaled with purpose and a smile. My proverbial shell hardened.

Before I could let my shell crack in the privacy of my room. Before I had to get ready for the cocktail party. Before I had to mingle in a room with Sonia for the first time since she kicked me out of her life...

I needed to survive this brunch.

CHAPTER SEVEN

Sonia

Out of necessity, I kept my gaze trained on Tallia, thankful to Stacy for the last-minute packet. Mentally cycling through bacheloress facts applicable to the moment, I fought the urge to turn to see if Elly was watching. Leaning in to my emergency department nurse nerves of steel, I exhaled a steady breath and focused on the person in front of me.

Tallia shook the crushed ice in her glass loose and tipped it up to sip the remnants.

"Here, have mine," I said, offering my cocktail, intending to stay sober. I needed a clear mind. And to get this brunch over with so I could find Elly and talk somewhere private.

The host said there were four ex-couples at the villa and four contestants completely unattached, for a total of twelve contestants and Tallia. We were free to be ourselves, which included pursuing connections in the villa outside of Tallia. For the exes, the decision to rekindle a flame, pretend it never existed, or anything else was theirs alone. Other than feeling bad for whoever here dated LeeAnn, I didn't much care who did what.

I only cared that they didn't do Elly.

"I already like you," Tallia joked, reaching for my purple drink still on the silver platter at the center of the table, where I'd set it after I headed to the table for dear life.

One look.

That was all it took.

One look from Elly and I almost ate cobblestone.

That woman had a power over me I would never fully understand. No woman before or since her has had that effect on me. One look from her, and years of locked-up love thudded to life. I didn't realize how badly I had missed Elly-bolts, those moments when out of nowhere her presence shocked me awake, made me more present. Sometimes it was a look. Other times it was a statement or a whole stream of statements connected to one another that only she had a way of keeping me engaged with.

Everything she had to say, I wanted to hear. How she thought, how she felt, what she thought about what she felt. Her intelligence, watching her play with the complicated and the simple, like balls of yarn to a kitten, was another of her siren songs to my sailor ears.

And then there were her eyes, grounding and soaring, pools of earthy sediment with flecks of gold glinting in the sun. In the quiet of late-night candlelight cuddles on her couch, I used to imagine diving into her ever-shifting pools, only to realize they were wells I could swim through to access her soul. When she was angry or hurt, her irises darkened and dulled, as though the sediment churned and clouded her mind. Every new passionate thought or emotion she shared, I wished I could traverse to its root, deep in her soul. There, I knew, I would find what brought her eyes such color, where her well met her heart.

I needed to know what Elly wanted. Just the idea of it brought on an onslaught of emotions.

Imagining her and me together, alone, talking, I ached to make time move quicker. Already, I sensed the magnets we seemed to have embedded in us for one another, how they pulled for our bodies to close the distance. Giddiness thrummed through me like I was getting to be reunited with a long-lost best friend, and I couldn't wait to end our estrangement.

An estrangement I caused.

Like a roller coaster, my mind and body flew to new heights considering the serendipity of us both being here, together. Just as powerfully, the ride plummeted into despair. Between Elly and me, there would be no joyous reunion. Because of my decision a year ago.

I redirected my thoughts toward Tallia, the only current safe place for them. At least until I figured out what to do next while on a show about either the messiness of sapphic love, or the unique intimacy some sapphic couples experienced, and the redemptive love contained inside such vulnerability. I couldn't tell yet. Mainstream media didn't have the best track record when it came to representing the authentic depth of queer love.

"They told me to expect a twist early in the show's filming, but I couldn't have seen this one coming," Tallia said to someone at our table as she tapped my arm. "Thankfully, Sonia was kind enough to go without her lavender mimosa, so I could drown my sorrows."

Oh yeah, Tallia had a thing for certain types of drinks. It was in the packet.

"What did you think of that, by the way?" I asked, since I carried the drinks across the perils of cobblestone for our table, and it was the only thing I could think to say. "The lavender addition? Or have you had it before?"

"Well…" she said, eyeing me flirtatiously with a grin, as though she weighed her words. "No, I haven't had this kind of mimosa before, and it was okay, but I wouldn't order it."

I let out a laugh. "Okay, so then what would you have ordered?"

Every millisecond, my brain reminded me Elly was nearby and probably watching. I wondered if she missed my laugh.

Tallia laughed and placed her palm on my forearm. I fought the urge to wipe her hand from me, or at least look to make sure Elly wasn't getting the wrong idea.

"A lemon drop," she stated. "The drink, not the shot."

Elly's go-to drink. Even hearing the name of it brought back happy memories.

"Good to know," was all I could say while a whole world of possibilities between Elly and me unfolded in my imagination.

Every step of this trip brought me face-to-face with Elly connections, until it placed me in front of her and asked if we wanted to try again. In Madrid, Spain, at a romantic villa. I couldn't help but wonder if my dad had anything to do with this. He always loved Elly and had a flair for theatrics. As far as dramatic reunions went, this one topped the cake.

Someone to the left of Tallia asked about her preference for ciders, as another original contestant stood from their table to approach ours.

As though that was our signal, people began to move away from their tables to socialize or whisper along the edges, away from the group. LeeAnn sat talking to the other woman at Elly's table, while my ex's seat sat empty.

I tried to inconspicuously sweep my gaze across the courtyard, in search of Elly. When I didn't see her, I lifted my head to look around. Still no Elly.

With enough people moving about the courtyard, I figured no one would think it strange if I went inside to look for Elly. I stood and started making my way toward the house when I realized I wasn't sure if I should go back the way I came, enter through the glass door, or maybe another way. The house was huge.

"Need help?" someone asked, and I turned to an outstretched arm with bright blue nails. "I'm Michelle, she her." She wore her shoulder-length hair wavy, barely shifting across her bare shoulders.

"I would very much appreciate the help," I admitted, releasing her handshake and offering for her to go first.

"I don't blame you," she started, as I followed her up stone steps to the back door. "I barely know how to get around this place. And tonight, after a few drinks, have fun finding your room. I'm just saying."

I opened the door, and she stepped in, changing the conversation midbreath from house size, to the kitchen's food and booze pantry, to bedroom locations. Katy stood at the far corner of the white-countered kitchen, her outfit a splash of color that didn't exactly match her facial expression as she shook her head when the woman she spoke to wiped a tear from her cheek.

Other than Katy and what looked to be her ex, and Michelle and me, the villa appeared to be empty. "Where are the bedrooms?" I asked my villa tour guide.

She gave a lazy wave toward the living room and what looked like a receiving room beyond that.

"Thanks," I said, making my way past a light brown couch. The living room held three.

Michelle didn't respond, and I didn't check to see why. A great wooden staircase revealed itself as I neared the entry of the house and recognized the arched double doors I had seen outside the villa when we first arrived.

Before I learned the real reason I was here. Before my dad led me back to Elly.

CHAPTER EIGHT

Elly

"You got this," I told my reflection in the framed mirror atop the dresser in my room, struggling for some solid knowing to cling to after the morning's brunch.

Existing in Sonia's sphere again brought reminders of what I lost when she walked away from *us*, single-handedly burying what I thought was a fated connection. Nestled in the proverbial casket beside the embalmed memory of us were the bones of my belief in fated souls.

My fingertips pressed into the wood as I glared at my reflection, daring myself to rise to the occasion. My version of a little black dress clung to my curves and stopped midthigh. Tiny sparkling gems formed little flowers from under my breast line to my waist. The gems dispersed like petals on the wind down the sheer length of ethereal blue fabric nearly reaching my painted toes. Quartz petal earrings hung from each lobe, another form of my love of flowers made obvious.

When I had packed this dress, I packed with it dreams of a new path, of true and lasting love. But my problems followed me. Onto a TV show of all places. Now I pitied myself in the mirror, deflated from whatever confidence I had when I came here.

Life had been hard since Sonia left me.

Over the phone.

During a fight.

Who would do that to the person they claimed to love? To the person they claimed to adore so much they wanted to marry them and grow old together?

When it first happened, I expected her to call back once she calmed. She had lost her dad months prior and grief's inevitable mood swings brought rough waters to our relationship, turbulent seas I intended to navigate with her, secure in our ability to lean on one another and grow in the process.

Out of everyone in the world, I wanted to be someone to *her*. She was my garden, where I found the most delight, where I sowed seeds and counted time by the cycles of seasons with no end. I used to get lost in brushing the back of her neck, where thick muscles connected to feminine lines, and gentle curves met strength. That's how I would define Sonia too, strength and heart.

And no longer mine.

Because Sonia never did end up calling me back.

Tears filled my eyes as I gazed into my own soul. Why did *she* have to be here? I was in Spain of all places. I read that ecotourism was big here. There were forests out there, full of history and folklore. Pristine beaches. And women, single, gorgeous, kind, smart women. Yet none of that called to me the way she did, the woman I wanted more than anything.

The woman who didn't want me.

I hated her for that.

My hometown of Spokane had become a lot smaller now that Sonia and I were done. I took great measure to avoid the one queer club in town she visited. And her neighborhood? Yeah, it had been my favorite, but now it was just a bunch of streets and businesses I drove through for work and nothing else.

It wasn't that I thought she'd be rude or even talk to me if we saw one another out in public. No, the roots of my hesitance grew deeper than that. Seeing her face pop up in my social media and phone memories was bad enough. Seeing her in person would have likely ripped my heart out and left me publicly speechless.

I laughed to myself, my eyes filled with angry tears now,

replacing my earlier sadness. Maybe seeing her on the set of a TV show was the universe's way of ripping the Band-Aid off.

Why, though? We were done. There was no point to us interacting, no use in tilling up rotting manure.

I gave myself a serious stare. Sonia and I were well past our expiration date, and entertaining romantic fantasies of us magically picking up where we left off was painfully futile. Unfortunately, some connections came with expiration dates.

I needed to stop thinking the universe had a master plan when it yanked me around by putting me with a woman who made it clear that I was not for her...after convincing me I was everything she wanted.

"Okay," I told myself, pushing from the dresser to stand proudly. "I never needed her."

I shook out my hands, working to lessen the tension.

I inhaled to fill my lungs, held it for five seconds, and then slowly blew it out. Each time I repeated this, my shoulders eased down a little more. I wanted to cry at the thought of Sonia being here as the reason my shoulders were tensed. When would I get to escape this tender topic? When would I be able to move on with my life? When would Sonia just be someone I used to know?

The loud knock shocked me out of my thought loop. I turned to stare at the bedroom door, my mind spinning.

Sonia?

My heart beat wildly against my chest. I opened my mouth to gasp in a breath of air and swallow it down, fighting tears from spilling over. What if I was wrong? What if she missed me?

I hurried to the door, only to freeze at arm's length. If Sonia knocked at my door, it was to talk alone with me, probably to make sure I kept us a secret so she could pursue Tallia.

My heart fell to my feet. Preparing for the fresh cut of rejection from Sonia, I exhaled and swung the door open, ready to get the familiar anguish over with.

Sapphire stood in front of me. Her mermaid-cut dress extended from strappy shoulders to a wave of bluish-green shiny fabric reaching the floor. Her blond hair sat atop her head in a poofy bun, with ringlets of blond framing her expertly made-up face.

"Oh!" I exclaimed, my jumbled thoughts clearing to form a sentence. "You are the most beautiful mermaid I have ever laid eyes on." I placed my hand on my chest like a proud big sister.

"Really?" she asked with a squee, turning to give me the full experience. "I wasn't sure."

"Let me be sure for both of us, then." I laughed tightly and slid my high heels on. "You ready to head down?"

Sapphire's smile dimmed, and instead of turning to lead the way, she took a step into my room, and then another, and closed the door behind her.

She sat in the armchair in the corner of my room, beside the standing full-length mirror, between the glass balcony door and my dresser. She crossed her legs, exposing her matching shiny fish scale heels.

"You seriously went for the mermaid theme tonight," I said, painfully aware that was my second comment on the topic of her outfit. But I had to say something, and that was the first thing that popped into my head.

"Too much?" she asked, pointing her open-toed shoes to reveal toenails covered in blueish-green scales.

I smiled, thankful that she went along with my distraction. "Mermaids? Never."

"You want to talk about brunch?" she asked.

I let my happy mask slip. My shoulders dropped. Could she tell I saw my ex today? Or did she want to tell me she saw hers?

I was not, in fact, ready to share my private inner thoughts with a near stranger. What if, of the two of us, I was the only one with an ex here?

"The show's twist just got me thinking about my ex," I offered.

Sapphire gave a knowing nod as her knitted brows softened her expression with empathy. "Tonight is going to be tough for a lot of us," she said, her voice sullen, serious.

Everything in me wanted to let go of my heavy secrets. Wanted to let her know what seeing Sonia's tattooed forearms did to me, and how, when it came to Sonia, something as simple as that had the power to unravel me.

I used to trace those tattoos. Used to press passionate lips against the ones hidden under fabric on her shoulders and upper biceps. Used to know, with everything in me, that the Harriet Beecher Stowe quote, vertical up the back of her left bicep, meant we were made for one another.

I remembered the first time I spotted the quote in Old English calligraphy—*Women are the real architects of society*—the day I met Sonia at a queer sapphic prom in Seattle.

The hot masc brunette had been standing in line to get carded and a bracelet, about ten people in front of me and my group of friends.

That was the first time I noticed her. She wore dark charcoal slacks and a black button-up under a deep purple vest with her freshly cut fade. Everything about the way she carried herself, as though she belonged there, and how sharply put together she dressed caught my attention.

My group and I had gotten to the venue a little later than planned and ended up having to wait for the rush of people before us, before the line started moving. I had noticed Sonia when I first got in line, then went back to listening to a friend talk about the girls she hoped to meet that night.

But it was when Sonia's friend group neared the ID checkpoint podium that she released her left cufflink and rolled her sleeve up to reveal a tanned, tattooed arm. I had been totally there with my friends, present in the moment, while also absolutely consumed by the words trailing down the glowing skin of a woman in a group ahead of me.

I had become aware of two things standing in line, that unsuspecting May evening. One: I was going to make it my mission to find the person belonging to that arm, and learn what inspired its ink. And two: That night would be one for the books, a kind of magic worthy of the emerald-green floor-length dress I wore.

Those moments I would never get back were ghosts long gone, parading through my heart as the living. I wondered if what I had with Sonia would always be seared into my skin as a thin layer of scab barely protecting the brokenness underneath. Would the bump of her scent or whisper of her voice always cause it to ooze pain?

I had hoped coming on to this show would be the medicine I needed to progress that thin scab to healed skin, growing thicker by the month.

A new sense of panic took root in my belly and brought a wave of tears.

Sapphire walked over to stand beside me in front of the mirror. She slid a delicate hand from my shoulder down my arm and backed me slowly to my mattress. We sat at the end of my bed, facing the dresser.

My whispered words slipped out. "I miss her so much."

I inhaled sharply, as though each string of breath was a thread sewing my feelings back into place.

"Oh, honey." She leaned in. "It's like grief. When you think you've gotten over them, along comes a memory or a scent or, fuck, seeing a certain kind of bird, and bam! It's like they just left and you're reeling."

I gulped and gave a shaky exhale.

I wished I could breathe out my emotions, rid them into the ether, never to be felt again.

I leaned my temple onto her shoulder and focused on the bronze dresser knob across from us, to keep my pain from becoming tears.

"It's wrong to start a new relationship with someone when I'm still having moments of reeling from my ex, though," I stated, an old fear resurfacing from the last time I tried to date and only compared them to her.

People liked to spout quotes about getting under someone to get over someone to the newly brokenhearted. If the connection was shallow, sure, a new shallow connection could do wonders at washing away the old one.

What we had wasn't shallow, though. Romantic distractions were powerless to dislodge Sonia from her throne in my heart.

What if I couldn't get over Sonia? Would I stay single? Would I never again get to plug myself into another soul and allow love to light me up?

Sapphire narrowed her eyes. "Is it, though? Is it wrong to try with someone new?"

I raised my gaze from the dresser knob to look at Sapphire's reflection in the mirror above the dresser.

"I think it is," I said. "I wouldn't want to get feelings for someone who isn't over their ex."

"Are you not over your ex?" she countered. "Or are you sometimes grieving the loss of them in your life? I think there's an important difference."

I hadn't considered it that way. I sat up straighter on the bed and turned to look her in the face. "How can I tell if I'm not over her or if it's just grief?" Helping others tackle these types of questions was my bread and butter. When it came to matters of my own heart, though, clinical knowledge flew out the window.

"I think grief is a sadness that eases with time but can also bite you out of nowhere." She pulled a blond ringlet from her glossy lip and placed it back on the side of her face where it belonged. "Its bite doesn't mean it's constantly in your life, weighing on you. It means you got bit and the swelling will ease and you'll be fine."

"I guess," I said. "Maybe." I mentally chewed on her perception.

The corners of Sapphire's lips turned up as she eyed me. "We're BFFs here, mermaids on an island of seagulls and crabs."

I couldn't help but smile at that one. I shook my head in a slow, half-assed way that said *You're crazy* and also *Thank you*.

How could I tell where my Sonia grief stopped and my Sonia yearning started? I ached to rest my head on her shoulder, to feel her arms wrapped around me, to breathe her in.

And yet was that all just grief? It had to be feelings of missing her, right? It had to be that I wasn't over her yet. And if I wasn't over her yet, why the hell was I here?

The idea bloomed in my mind like a dandelion while squeezing my heart with its invasive root. I had to talk to Sonia. And not in the fantastical way my imagination conjured, like a weighted blanket to calm my panic.

We could be rational adults for five minutes and leave emotions out of it. We needed to be on the same page about keeping us a secret.

I caught my heart smiling at the idea of us forming a pact to protect one another secretly in the house, feeding the information of others to each other. Like a team.

No, we weren't together, building webs of strategy, sharing information to help one another. Hell, we weren't even friends.

I didn't need to create more fantasies about Sonia. Too many of my hopes and dreams with Sonia went up in flames and then were left to rot. We didn't end because of some huge betrayal. No one lied. No one cheated. No one got a new job and had to leave town.

According to Sonia, I no longer cared about her feelings or our relationship.

That was the knife that severed what we were. And then metaphorical swords were drawn. Metaphorical blood was spilled. Real hearts were broken. Real dreams were murdered.

Now, Sonia and me being enemies was more than metaphorical.

"Okay. Grief." I stood from the edge of the bed and smoothed the flowy fabric of my dress over my hips. "This too shall pass," I said, repeating a favored saying of mine. Thanks to time, everything passed. If we used the time with intent, it would bring healing and comfort.

"That's the stuff," Sapphire said brightly. If her ex was among the new contestants, she didn't seem to be too upset by it. She stood behind me, pretended to dust off my shoulders and fluff my hair. "You said you were a therapist, right?"

"I am," I said. And then added, "Why?" because of a sudden fear of being judged for asking questions I should know the answers to.

Taking one last look in the mirror, I inwardly hyped myself

up to go downstairs with my head held high. The desire to be as far from Sonia and cameras as possible entangled with the need to forge ahead and not let others detour me from what I wanted. I promised myself not to allow the entanglement to trip me up.

Later, I would poke through the flurry of my emotions in the privacy of my bedroom, with my journal. For now, I would stride through the halls with Sapphire and try my hardest to live in the moment. To be present. To be fearless.

"You ready?" I asked, opening my bedroom door for Sapphire.

We made our way down the hall. Little square windows lined the outer wall, overlooking an inner side garden. During the day, shades of green, in the leaves of bushes and plants, framed a walkway. At night, the walkway disappeared from view and twinkle lights emerged. I made a mental note to wander the property and find that garden.

Between each pair of windows hung a square painting, nearly the same size as the windows, of flora and fauna that I assumed once occupied the grounds. One painting included a villa fountain behind a multicolored peacock.

Sapphire looped her arm in mine as we walked, descending the stairs to the first floor.

I allowed myself to trust her footing long enough to look up at the ceiling and then down to the floor. Thick dark wooden beams, one after the other, lined the ceiling. Just gazing up, one could imagine themselves walking this villa when it had first been constructed, or a little later, preparing to make their way to the gardens to paint.

I came here for a reason, I thought, noticing how the new and the old of the villa created its own tapestry of art.

At the landing beneath us lay a huge oval rug. Patterns of deep green stems stretched out to hook and wind together, blotted with pastel splotches, flower petals against a deep red backdrop. It reminded me of an Expressionist painting—shapeless and formless colors from up close, but from farther up the stairs, it boasted a beautiful representation of nature's perfect chaos.

I wondered if that was the approach I should take over the next few days and weeks. Maybe I needed to think of this time on the show as splotches because I was too close. Maybe letting them be random colors for now was okay, because with enough distance and time, I would eventually see I was weaving a masterpiece.

Yeah, that felt right.

Chapter Nine

Sonia

I stepped in from the pool patio, for the third time since the cocktail party began, searching for Elly. I needed us to talk before things got started—she needed to know how I felt. My earlier attempts to find her room only showed me more of the villa and probably made me look strange, wandering aimlessly.

A white granite counter, extending half the width of the room, separated the living room from the kitchen. Two original contestants blended drinks in one corner of the kitchen. A group of four, including Katy, stood on the other side, the counter an island between the groups who seemed to keep to their own little circles' conversations.

I moved along the granite toward the villa's entrance and stairway.

Two-thirds of the contestants at the villa had the luxury or detriment of knowing someone else here. I wondered if one of the people in Katy's group was her ex. Which exes saw this as an opportunity to have a familiar face far from home, and which felt like their heaven just turned to hell?

As if she walked out of a solid wall in the entrance area, Elise swooped in and cut me off from checking the second-floor hall of bedrooms again.

"Good evening." She seemed to sing the words. "Do you mind?" She extended her arm to motion us back into the living room and toward the arch past the kitchen. From my villa adventures earlier, I knew the arch led through to a dining room that led to a great room. Elly had been in neither.

I led the way, curious what Elise wanted to talk about so close to listening ears. Unlike earlier, the formal dining room looked like a pop-up dessert shop, the table full of edible decorations. It smelled like one too.

Elise opened her hand as though she was unwrapping a gift. A silver chain necklace attached to a black dog charm lay in her palm. "Here," Elise said, suddenly turning her open hand toward the floor.

I caught the jewelry in time.

She pulled a black cellphone from her jeans, typed for less than a second, and then slid it back. "Sorry," she said. The producers were constantly dealing with ten things at once on their phones, in their earpieces, and around them. It reminded me of the emergency department. I knew it was the demand of their job and nothing personal.

"This is your official show mic," she explained. "Unless you're in the restroom or your bedroom, you need to be wearing it at all times."

At this morning's brunch we had all worn clip-on mics and battery packs.

I fastened the silver chain around my neck. "Thanks."

Elise smiled and checked her phone again.

I looked to our right, toward the hall leading to the game room. The newly folded paper in my pocket could have been a combustible package, the way it demanded I hand it off to its rightful owner. Maybe Elly had gone into the game room while I was outside looking for her.

The creation of what I had scrawled on the folded paper came from the desire to ignite, not to tear apart.

At the lowest point in my pit of grieving the losses of my dad and Elly, in an attempt to find release, I had revisited an art form I'd loved as an angsty teen and dabbled with in college—poetry.

After the brunch, I tore a page from my journal and rewrote a poem I had sitting at home on my laptop in my folder titled *Her*. I hoped Elly would let me read it to her.

Seeing her made me feel alive. Something about Elly's presence breathed new life into me. She had always said we were soulmates, fated to be together. I used to not believe in stuff like that, spiritual connections. My dad's sudden death confirmed for me that the whole loving spirit world idea was a bunch of bullshit. How could it be true if a person who lived a life of acceptance and love was erased from existence like he never mattered?

I couldn't wait to tell Elly how everything on this trip felt like signs leading me to her. More than anything, I wanted to feel her frame's weight against my body, inhale her scent, wrap around her soft skin, and tell her she's my soulmate. That I believed now.

"Is that all?" I asked, impatience slipping through my voice.

Elise looked up from her phone long enough to give an appreciative smile and nod, then left for the kitchen, toward the back patio doors.

Thankful for the briefness of the interaction, I double-checked no one could see me and hurried down the short, silent hall full of watercolor paintings of plants. Swinging one of the plain double doors open, I was met by a quiet, dark game room, its carpeted expanse unpopulated.

"Nope," I said, turning on my heel to close the door behind me.

"Sonia! They want us outside," Katy called from the kitchen.

By the time I got through the dessert-filled dining room, the kitchen and living room were empty of contestants. That meant Elly was likely outside too. Everything—down to the fact that out of all my colognes, I'd brought Elly's favorite scent—told me I was here for Elly.

As I neared the back doors, I slowed my pace and cleared my throat in hopes of directing my next uttered words at my ex. I could cry with excitement. It all made so much sense now.

Elly stood on the other side of the glass doors, maybe thirty feet away, scanning the rainbow wine cart. Plexiglass bottle holders perched along the bar, each a different height, gave the illusion of floating wines. Rainbow lights illuminated the display from under the clear plexiglass countertop.

When I had been on the patio searching for her before, I passed by the cart and thought about how it would make her smile. I hadn't considered what she would be wearing while smiling that sunshine of a smile.

She looked like...her. Like my Elly, a crown of golden hair pulled up to expose a shaved undercut. My little fairy in her dark ethereal dress, sparkling like the stars in the sky tonight. I nearly lost my breath, standing so close, getting to see her without her seeing me. A surge of adoration welled in my chest. I inwardly thanked my dad again.

Elly grabbed a bottle from the cart and said something to LeeAnn, who I now noticed crouched at the darkened base under the lit bar. LeeAnn offered a wineglass from under the bar and stood. Her black pinstripe pantsuit matched her black sequined crop top, and like earlier, she wore her shoulder-length hair in a tight ponytail at the base of her skull.

I paused from opening the door to contemplate and prepare for what I was about to walk out to.

LeeAnn brandished a wine opener and Elly gave her the dark bottle, also offering the empty glass to fill. LeeAnn popped the cork and poured the light liquid until Elly thanked her, lifted it to her nose to inhale, and sipped.

It was adorable how Elly acted like a wine snob after one girls' trip to central Washington's wine country. She had been new to wine tasting and only liked sweet white wines. I wondered if what LeeAnn poured was a sweet wine, or if Elly's palate had matured while we were apart.

I watched the way she laughed and pressed her fingers to LeeAnn's exposed bicep for a short moment. The way she eyed my poor excuse for a stand-in over the glass's rim as she sipped. Did I see a sparkle in her gaze for LeeAnn, someone else's ex, and probably the woman here least like me?

I figured Elly had changed a little since we broke up, like everyone does. But it occurred to me, she could have changed a lot.

In the last year, I felt like I found myself. What if she did too? And what if her newer version of self wanted women like LeeAnn, not like me? She had a right to pursue her happiness, even if it didn't include me.

Smoothing down the front of my shirt, I opened one of the double doors and stepped onto the patio. I neared the wine cart, opposite Elly and LeeAnn, with every intention of remaining invisible long enough to make it into a cluster of people. Before walking out into the garden courtyard this morning, after they shared the twist of navigating this show beside our exes, I wholly intended to treat Elly like a formidable ex.

Then I saw her, and possibilities rose from nowhere, like items pulled into a tornado. Now others joined the storm. Elly could have already moved on. She could be a different person, and not my type.

The show host's booming voice stopped me from slinking away without Elly noticing. I froze.

Shit, they were filming.

Elly and LeeAnn stood close enough to brush bare shoulders, looking away from me and toward the poolside corner of the property where Kamal spoke. The illuminated cart stood between them and me, as I waited for a break in filming to sneak away.

I couldn't consider Elly falling for LeeAnn. I refused to believe she was capable of trusting someone who didn't recognize that a trail of failed short-term relationships equaled a pattern pointing back to herself. Elly was too emotionally mature for someone like LeeAnn.

Mostly, though, I couldn't let the reality of Elly falling for anyone permeate my thoughts. Not right now. Not with her poem in my pocket.

CHAPTER TEN

Elly

I stood beside LeeAnn at the rainbow-decorated wine cart, aerating my Riesling while watching Kamal introduce Tallia. They bantered about her experience christening the confessional room. He hinted at her confessing her top three choices. She insisted she didn't have a top five yet, let alone three.

A quick sniff of the contents in my glass confirmed the swirling paid off. Sweet pear notes met my tongue first, followed by green apple. The summery Riesling I sipped gave me hope that my attempts of numbing my Sonia pain tonight would be met with delicious ease.

Since arriving at the villa, I hadn't spent time on this pool patio, not to be confused with the garden patio or the various gardens themselves. Tonight's party, with candles, a rock fire table, and twinkly garden lights, gave the fun, flirty, romantic vibe.

It made me think of Sonia, who I didn't see when I came out. I still nearly turned down LeeAnn's offer to show me the wine cart, worried my ex would see and get the wrong idea. Although I couldn't be sure what that wrong idea would be at this point. And I didn't hate the idea of her witnessing LeeAnn's attention. Not after having to watch her with Tallia earlier today, like I didn't exist. A message I heard loud and clear.

Hesitance struck me, and I paused from gazing at the flickering flames floating in the pool. A small group stood at a table across the pool. I decided not to squint enough to see the shadowed faces of the table's occupants. If Sonia caught me looking for her, I'd be mortified. I snuck a sly look around the pool patio to find her.

Thankful for the warmth spreading through my body, I reminded myself to slow my pace on the alcohol, not to give in to the allure of letting go.

One of the shadowed faces across the water belonged to Sonia. The height and athletic build looked right, around five foot six or so. Mostly it was the way the silhouette carried her shoulders back and held her chin up just enough to convey a humble confidence.

Knowing where not to look, I focused on the unfolding drama everyone else watched. Not only did Tallia barely have a top five, but she also loathed the idea of contestants dating with their exes present. "Unfair," she called it.

If my hand wasn't occupied with liquid deliciousness, I would have clapped with a couple of the others who agreed with our bacheloress.

My mind wandered to Sonia again. I imagined her sneaking glances at me each chance she got. She used to joke when I talked about wine, called me a weekend connoisseur. At the time I took it as a compliment about how quickly I picked up wine tasting. After she told me that she had realized we weren't a good fit after all, I added *talking about wine* to the list of possible things she secretly hated about me.

What if watching me swirl my glass and sniff and sip reminded her that I was a wine snob? I breathed into the sudden side cramp and lengthened the left side of my body, enough to stretch the pain out of existence without catching anyone's attention.

The shadowed figure of Sonia looked right at me.

I pretended to focus on Tallia and Kamal. Pretended not to care that she was looking right at me. She wanted me to see. My chest tightened with an anxious want I knew too well.

What would she say if she knew I cried about her to Sapphire upstairs? If she knew how hard it was to come to terms with the fact that no one else could be her, and I couldn't be with her, and how unfair it all felt.

"Tonight is about new beginnings," Kamal proclaimed as he and Tallia made their way from the area with stationary lights to a darkened corner, where a single spotlight switched on to focus on the two. "Tallia has refined her selection. Now is the time to intentionally get to know her, let her get to know you. Or to work things out with your ex, a choice not everyone here gets."

He whispered into Tallia's ear while a couple cameras panned over the contestants, huddled in groups and couples. She left his side and disappeared into the dark corner.

"For tonight's cocktail party," Kamal continued, "you can find our lovely bacheloress here, in her private lounge, enjoying her favorite handmade cocktails." A chandelier hanging from the branch of a mature tree flickered to life above and behind him. Faux fires danced in place along the tops of three rings hovering over one another.

Tallia's yellow skirt took on a glowy hue, as she was sitting directly under the firelight in the secluded corner. She lounged on a dark wicker chaise, a matching love seat across from her, both seats covered in red cushions.

"Will you hit it off over drinks and common interests?" Kamal asked the crowd, as he neared the black outdoor rugs between the chairs in Tallia's space. "Or will you choose to spend your time getting reacquainted with your ex? Choose wisely, the fate of your experience at the villa depends on it." Our host looked over the crowd with an expectant smile.

Using her hand to cover her eyes enough to keep the chandelier light from blocking her view, Tallia scanned the contestants. "I don't have a drink," she said on a laugh.

"Well then, let me fix that," Sonia responded from directly behind me, playfully, with her distinct hint of rasp in her voice. "Lemon drop, right?"

Hot tears sprang to my eyes.

I clenched my jaw and stared forward, pretending not to keep track as she moved away from the wine cart toward the back doors.

She wasn't the silhouette at a table on the opposite side of the pool. She had been standing feet away from me, watching from behind, like I was a stranger. Probably judging the way I drank my Riesling.

I didn't need to look to see Sonia's dark hair and faded sides, with enough length on top to look perfectly tousled. I wondered what outfit she chose for tonight and automatically wished I could feel the fabric pressed between us, wished I could breathe in her cologne.

I automatically inhaled. Hard. Fresh tears threatened to spill from the corners of my eyes. Of all the cologne bottles lining her bathroom counter, she chose to bring my favorite. To lure another woman.

Tallia giggled, her smile nothing short of absolute delight.

While my stomach folded in on itself in utter disenchantment.

"That would be perfect," she answered with a wink and a smile that didn't belong to Sonia. "You remember how I like it—the drink, not the shot."

My go-to cocktail was now a drink order Sonia remembered for another woman. If I needed to see proof Sonia was capable of replacing me, here it was.

"On it!" my ex-fiancée responded before leaping to assist the bacheloress.

It didn't take a dictionary to interpret Sonia's message. I barely saw her out of my peripheral vision, but I got it loud and clear. She was deciding to invest her time in Tallia. Not me. I was her past, not her present, and certainly not her future.

I willed my tears to go back where they came from. The moment I heard the door shut behind Sonia, I looked around to make sure no one spotted my emotional slipup. Questions were the last thing I needed.

I didn't have answers to give. Not when my ex flitted around flirting in front of me, uncaring of how hard I fought the mental and physical barriers to be here, just to be thwarted by her every damn time I came downstairs.

Among my reasons for coming to Spain, watching Sonia hurry to bring another woman a lemon drop wasn't one of them.

"Bullshit," I uttered under my breath. The word summed it up, how I felt about Sonia yet again gifting me with a twisting, burning pain from my stomach to my heart.

She knew I was here too, watching, hearing.

While she was inside mixing Tallia's requested cocktail, Sonia had to be getting a special kind of joy from the added gut punch of the fact that she was bringing Tallia the same drink she used to bring me.

In front of me.

When Sonia jogged back outside, she stayed fixed on Tallia. A sturdy hand carrying the coveted lemon drop, complete with a sugar rim, entered my view. We all got to witness their eyes lock as Sonia neared Tallia's lounge and presented her with a beautiful, and probably delicious, handmade cocktail.

I bet she took great joy in adding her signature drop of lavender oil or a sprig of lavender. With the show's whole sapphic vibe, she wouldn't have any trouble finding lavender. The house was decorated with purple flowers, including tall, narrow vases of dried lavender stalks. A close study of the glass showed she chose not to go with the sprig. Maybe she found edible essential oils in the kitchen like I had in mine.

Sonia was dressed to perfection in silver-gray slacks, fitted enough to show her cute butt, and a tapered black button-up with a violet tie. The sleeves on her shirt were rolled up to beneath her elbows, displaying my favorite quotes on her forearms.

Tallia accepted the sweating glass as her face lit up like the dancing flames above their heads. If she hadn't been before, Sonia was definitely now in Tallia's top five.

"Well, well!" Kamal laughed, making his way into the private lounge. "Looks like the early bird really does get the worm." He dramatically eyed the glass. "How is it?" he asked Tallia.

She took a steady sip, all eyes on her, and swallowed. Immediately a new smile spread across her face, showing off a row of perfect teeth.

Sonia loved a girl with good dental hygiene.

"It's delicious!" she announced before resting a hand on Sonia's forearm and taking another sip.

Eventually, Tallia was going to run her fingers along the outlines of Sonia's tattooed inscriptions. She was going to ask Sonia about them over a romantic dinner, or while naked in Sonia's arms, and be swept up by the stories. She was going to fall in love with Sonia.

I could throw up.

Contestants clapped and laughed.

I was in hell.

This was hell, right?

"I'm gonna need something a little harder than wine, I think," I whispered under my breath to LeeAnn.

She gave a quick half smile and returned her attention to Tallia and Kamal.

And Sonia. Who I could now no longer avoid looking at without being obvious.

Eyeing my empty glass, I glanced at the different carts in search of something stronger. Whiskey wasn't my thing. But I knew for a fact there was a bottle of Tito's in the kitchen.

I didn't bother mentioning anything to LeeAnn before I checked to make sure all eyes were on the happy couple and slipped inside the house.

CHAPTER ELEVEN

Sonia

Halfway between Tallia's lounging corner for the evening and the patio hosting tonight's cocktail party, I crested a small grassy knoll. Behind me sat the bacheloress and the contestant who interrupted us.

Ahead of me, two people talked in tense, hushed tones in an adjacent darkened corner at the far front end of the property. Branches from the row of privacy trees behind them and tall bushes beside them concealed their discussion. A small group sat around the tabletop fire, discussing show strategy. Candles floated in the kidney-shaped pool, bobbing from the rock wall water feature's disturbances when they wandered too close.

Elly must have gone inside, I decided and continued past the rainbow wine cart, walking into the house through the double doors from the patio. I stood in the empty living room, lit only from the can lights pointed at large impressionist wall art. Dance music boomed down the hall from the game room.

I listened for Elly's laugh for half a second before losing patience and heading for the dining area. Before I turned past the end of the granite countertop and swung a right from the kitchen to the dining area, the sheer light blue of Elly's dress floated on a breeze swung up from the opening door of the confession room.

As if she was the dancing flame, and I the moth, I found myself inhaling her hippie-herbal scent without the cognitive decision to go to her. I stood steady on the uneven entrance tiles, my right hand on the doorknob to the confessional room.

Elly, eyes wide and chin tilted up, also had her hand on the door's knob, the other side. We stood still, frozen in a moment I doubted either of us saw coming. A moment growing larger by the passing milliseconds, filling to burst.

Her stubborn eyes stayed locked onto mine from the moment she looked up and saw me standing on the other side of the door. Like an ever-shifting puzzle matrix, emotions flashed across her light brown irises, and through the knitting and unknitting of her brow.

Actual thoughts didn't exist in this moment, our moment. How could they compete with the absolute takeover of repressed need?

When her chest rose hard and fast, when her lips opened for a gasp, when they closed on an audible cry, the kind that crawled from the depths of pain, I wrapped my left arm around her waist to stabilize her. I pushed us both into the small room and shut the door.

A salt lamp lit the narrow space in a dull orange glow, shielding me from seeing much. I held her against me, my nose in her hair, her breath on my shoulder. Tears wound down my cheeks and fell onto the crown of her head. I couldn't believe I was holding Elly. My Elly.

The reality of the moment burst inside like fireworks. I never thought I would get to feel her again. A sob wracked me, and my knees gave out.

Together, we crumbled to the floor, our arms refusing to let go.

In the quiet darkness filled with muffled sobs, I pulled her onto my lap and squeezed her closer. This woman, she was my everything. Her fingers pressed into my sides as though she clawed for me. I wished I could melt into her, become one being, so I would never have to leave her presence again.

I fucked up when I let her go. I let go of my everything and hadn't been the same since. Without Elly, life just didn't sparkle the same. Colors lost their burst. Food lost its flair. Elly brought flavor to my life in ways I couldn't fathom until she was gone.

Bringing my right hand up her back, through her long hair, to the base of her skull, I tilted her face to mine. Our mouths neared hesitantly before a soft test of a kiss.

Elly inhaled on a sob. She pulled away enough for me to see the sheen of tears glimmering in her eyes, their streams gliding down her cheeks.

I couldn't think enough to speak. She exhaled on a whimper, and I placed both hands behind her head, lowering myself to meet her lips with the passion burning a hole through me with want for this woman. Only this woman.

Her mouth opened, and I groaned in response, eager to be as close and connected to Elly as possible. Entangling my tongue with hers, I lowered my hand onto the small of her back and clutched her to me. If I could drink from the fountain of Elly the rest of my life, I would be a blessed human.

"Baby," she cried into my ear after pulling out of our kiss to reposition herself on me.

That's all I needed.

With my arm still around her waist, I pulled her frame from the floor and tucked her up into my embrace, carrying her to the love seat. Gently setting her down, I placed her head on the cushioned arm of the couch. My forearm tucked under her neck, I straddled Elly, my knees pressed into cushions. My heart beat wildly.

She grabbed my neck and forced me into her. I let go and allowed my weight to press into her as her legs wrapped around my waist, the sheer panels of her dress falling to the side.

I buried my nose into her neck and inhaled my favorite oxygen, kissing every centimeter of skin within reach. She tilted her head, giving me access. Elly moaned for more before grabbing the back of my head again and tangling her tongue with mine.

Greedily, I took whatever she wanted to give.

Wave after wave of need, joy, and fear rushed over me, knocking my thoughts into undiscernible fragments.

Elly pushed her torso up and leaned on an elbow, shoving her chest into mine, her nails digging into my ass through my dress slacks. That was all I needed to crawl my fingers up her smooth, strong thigh, toward her hip. I so missed her hips.

"Mmm, baby," Elly moaned while trailing kisses down the side of my neck. "Touch me."

"I'm here," I said before kissing her head. "I'm not going anywhere."

She grabbed my hand from her thigh and placed it between her legs. "Touch me."

I froze.

It wasn't that everything in my body didn't demand I do exactly that, touch her. All of her. But she meant more to me than our bodily demands. Our tears weren't even dry yet. We had a lot to unpack before sex.

It wasn't like Elly to rush straight to the physical, especially after everything that went on between us. She usually had to cool off after any type of argument before cuddling with me. She called it her regulation time.

I leaned on my arms to hold me above her, pulling us apart. She released her hold on me. Her soft expression hardened as she looked up at me.

"What?" she asked dryly.

I jumped off her and stood above the love seat, shocked. My thoughts knocked into each other as I stared down at a version of Elly I didn't remember. She fumbled with her dress strap, sat up, and smoothed her hair.

"Ah well, that stint was quick, wasn't it?" she said with a huff and stood.

She lost her footing and stumbled sideways toward a little round side table. The vodka bottle came into view as I lunged forward to help her. She slapped at the air, and I lost my balance trying not to get swatted.

She must have noticed me eying the bottle on the side table, because she turned to see where I looked. "Oh! There it is," she said.

Clutching the bottle to her chest, she made her way out of the room.

"What are you doing?" I asked, confused. Two minutes ago she insisted I touch her, and now she was leaving?

She ignored me and kept walking. Her heel caught on a tile every few steps. I jogged to her and stayed within arm's reach.

"Are you going to bed?" I said, trying to get an idea of what was happening.

"Where else would I go?" she asked, like I would know.

But now I knew she was leading me to her room, which I could work with.

"How much have you had to drink tonight?" I said, collecting information to determine my next steps.

She climbed the great staircase, clinging to the rail and the exposed wood portion of the steps to stay away from what I assumed was the tripping hazard of the runner down the center. I stayed two steps lower, ready to catch her.

As if she read my mind, she said, "Don't act like you're going to catch me or anything. I already know better."

I paused on a step as she continued to carefully make her way up.

"What's that supposed to mean?" I asked, offended. "I would absolutely catch you, even if it meant we'd both go down. At least I'd break your fall."

She scoffed. "It's a cute fantasy, but we've both seen how untrue that is."

At the top, on the last step, her heel caught on the rug. She swung for balance with her free arm.

I ran up the stairs, grabbed the banister for anchoring support with one hand, and reached to catch her.

In all her drunk girl glory, Elly turned long enough to glare at me the moment she righted herself and ripped her heel from the snag. Painfully slowly, she moved from the stairway to the hallway, keeping a palm against some part of the house the entire time.

Once she righted herself, free of any wall help, she sang down to me, "I've got it," followed up by a dry, "Learned how to catch myself after you pulled the rug out from under me. I'm a pro now."

"Okay, enough," I said, closing the distance between us.

She ignored me, padding down the hallway. Bedroom doors

lined the wall to our left, and square windows dotted the plaster-looking wall on our right.

She swung a hard left, opening her bedroom door in the process. With a quick flick of her wrist, she flipped her lights on and proceeded to pace forward like she was headed toward a firing squad.

When we were together, she drank like this once a year, maybe twice. She had a thing for letting go at Kitty's bar downtown, where she said she felt safe to be free. It took two lemon drops to get her shaking it on the dance floor. It was damn cute too.

Back then, low walls and high flirtation made her eyes sparkle with a deceivingly innocent mischievousness when she drank. I could never stay away from her, especially when the only face she looked for from the dance floor was mine. The moment she found my face, every time, a smile would reach her eyes, the perfect mix of jovial and alluring. Like a fish caught on her hook, she drew me to her, an invisible line tying our bodies together under brick and strobe lights.

We weren't in Spokane anymore, though. And Elly wasn't mine. Kissing her in the confession room like we were able to just pick things back up was stupid. A year could change a person. It could have changed Elly. Probably did, in fact. For all I knew, Elly drank like this every weekend.

I closed her bedroom door behind me and locked it, out of habit.

Elly stood in front of her antique-looking bed, wooden columns at every corner reaching from the floor to the ceiling. "Don't act like you have a right to say you've had enough when I finally get the chance to tell you what I *really* think."

"Elly, you're literally clinging to a Tito's bottle, trying to say now's the time you want to finally tell me what you think?" I took a few steps and paused when I saw the flash of fear in her eyes.

"I get to decide when I say and what I say it," she said seriously.

If I wasn't terrified of hearing a year's worth of anger poured into words and stirred with vodka, I would have laughed at her word slipup.

I would have told her how cute she was.

I would have scooped her up and fallen onto the bed with her.

But it was the old version of Elly I wanted to do those things with, I reminded myself. I didn't know the new version.

"You're right," I conceded. The fact was I did end things, and not in the best way.

Her fidgeting stopped, and she narrowed her eyes just enough to give me the impression she heard me and didn't know what to make of it. "Thank you," was all she said. As though the steam keeping her agitation afloat escaped through those two words, she huffed and sat backward onto the bed.

She kicked off her shoes and looked down at the rug beneath her feet. "You know what the fucked-up part is?" She scoffed. "Even tonight, I wanted to drunk text you."

"What's the fucked-up part of that?" I asked. Me ending things with her had nothing to do with my love for her. She would always be safe with me. Maintaining a friendship with her hurt too much, but that didn't mean I wouldn't have been there for her at the drop of a hat in an emergency.

Elly lifted her chin and offered me a blank stare. "Well, the fact that I wanted to text you, for one."

"I don't see what's so wrong about wanting to text me," I said.

"Drunk texts are messy, not safe for exes," she answered. "It's a fact as classic as texting itself."

I gave myself a second to absorb her meaning and not her words. "Okay, but I'm not just any ex. I'm your ex-fiancée, who has never given you a reason to feel unsafe."

Whenever we went downtown at night, mostly to Kitty's bar, I kept an eye out for trouble to make sure I stood between the troublemaker and Elly. Shit, when we walked anywhere, I positioned myself as the one closest to traffic. Her safety always came first.

A harsh laugh exited her mouth, one I had never heard before. Like an axe, it chipped at my resolve for Elly, weakening my heart's vote to be with her and strengthening my list of reasons why it wasn't a good idea.

"You don't get access to my unfiltered anything," she seethed.

"Ha!" I heard myself responding. "And you got mad at me for not opening up after my dad died? Are you fucking serious?"

She blamed me for leaving her, for not being able to trust her during the hardest and most vulnerable time in my existence. When she refused to trust me with just a percentage of that kind of vulnerability? Double standard, much?

"Because it goes both ways," she yelled from her bed, flopping her hands beside her. The bottle of alcohol rolled away and then back onto her hand. She didn't seem to notice. "You've always tried to keep your life filtered and perfect, clean and tidy. It's not real, it's hiding. You hid from me our whole relationship, and when a huge thing happened, you couldn't hide anymore. So you left me. You ended it all. You ended us because when your only option was to let me in, you locked the fucking door."

"God." I nearly laughed to myself. "I can't believe I thought we could have an adult conversation without you twist—" I stopped myself. She wasn't twisting things, and I knew better than to say so, even if it felt like that in the moment.

"You think I'm twisting things because I have feelings that do not correspond with yours?" She gave a bitter laugh. "If that's not a red flag."

I stretched my shoulders and released an audible exhale, reminding myself not to fall into our old argument loop. A year in bereavement therapy had a way of shifting things into perspective.

"No, that's not it, I shouldn't have said that, that's not what I think," I said. Standing in the middle of her room felt awkward. Leaving would feel worse, though. I stuffed my hands in my pockets.

"Then what *do* you think?" she challenged.

"I think you don't understand," I said, simply.

Her scowl returned.

I kept going. "I think you haven't had the death of a parent and don't get the dark thoughts and excruciating pain, how it fractures your sense of who you thought you were and forces you to rebuild without them." Tears burned my eyes and blurred my vision. "And to be honest, as a trained therapist, I thought you would have known better."

That's what hurt most. If I was her client, she would have had more understanding, more grace. She would have patted me on the hand and told me how strong I was by attempting to give what little I had. Instead, she essentially told me it wasn't enough.

Unless I was at my best, I wasn't enough.

Elly's mask of anger broke. Her chest shuddered. Her throat shifted as she swallowed.

"And if you would have given me the chance, I would have been there for you," she said, an escaped tear dripping down her face.

But she hadn't been there for me. But telling her so tonight would be the opposite of helpful. We were at an impasse. I didn't know whether I should go to her or leave her. Both options felt wrong. Nothing felt right.

"I think I want to go to bed now," she said solemnly, answering my unvoiced question. "But first"—she held the bottle to her chest and unscrewed the cap for a hefty swig—"here's my drunk text, without actually having access to a phone." Lifting the bottle again, she took in another gulp, wiped her mouth, and screwed the cap back on.

Elly stood, wavering a little on her feet before gaining her full balance. Her messy blond hair looked windblown around her tear-stained face. Black makeup blurred and bled at the corners of her eyes. "I wish you weren't such a lighthouse to my heart. I'm sick of destroying myself on the rocky cliffs you use as protection."

A minute, maybe more, passed as we stared at one another. We stood two arms' lengths away, though it felt like universes lived between us. "I don't know how to fix this," I whispered into the gorge. "But I can see it's not happening tonight."

Like a statue, she gave no response.

"Can I at least take this downstairs for you?" I asked, nodding to the bottle she held dangling at her thigh.

She offered it up, and I closed the distance to take it, to breathe her in. My arms ached to wrap around her. My lips yearned to kiss hers. But that's how shattered love worked, right? No matter how hard the broken couple tried to forge forward across the bridge to one another, missing boards between them did more to remind them of the torturous fall below than the waiting arms of the other.

With a silent sigh, I left Elly's room. If she moved from where she stood, her shoulders dropped and her face sullen, it wasn't until after I shut the door behind me. I didn't bother returning the bottle to the kitchen. I couldn't risk rejoining the party downstairs. Plus, that wasn't why I asked for it.

Walking toward the stairs, I opened the last door on the right, my bedroom.

What a difference a year made.

Chapter Twelve

Elly

My head pounded as I pulled my bare feet into me on the oversized couch, one of a few couches in the living room.

It felt like a lazy morning after a house party. Most of us wore pj's. Mine were linen, the color and design as if red sneezed onto white. I smiled to myself, pleased with the comparison. It was what came to mind when I first saw the pants on the discount rack, my favorite spot in a store.

Sapphire and LeeAnn sat beside me on the couch, openly discussing last night's dessert layout between quiet snips of gossip. They started the conversation including me, but my lack of involvement must have led them to believe I wasn't interested.

I had one thing on my mind this morning, and so far, she was still upstairs.

Sapphire's voice quieted to barely a whisper and I listened closer. "So, I heard something juicy in the kitchen while I was waiting for a new pot of coffee to brew."

She waited. LeeAnn and I leaned in.

"Katy said she was outside the confession room last night and heard giggling and moaning. Like, the naked kind."

"No shit?" LeeAnn said, giving the confession room door new interest. "Did Katy see who it was?"

No one was waiting outside the room when Sonia and I left it last night. Not that I remembered. Everything had happened so fast. It felt like a tornado of repressed emotions spun up, touched down, and then vanished.

Sapphire shook her head.

My heart twisted in my chest with worry. I hadn't considered what Sonia did with her time after she left my room last night.

I pretended my battered heart wasn't beating at my ribcage for freedom from the pain of existing in Sonia's proximity. Her scent was the first thing I smelled when I woke. Absently reaching for her, only to find a cold spot of remembrance, sucked worse than waking up without coffee.

I wanted to bury my face in my hands, but I didn't. I fought myself to stay present, to be a part of this, to remember I was bigger than one aspect of my life, to not allow my inner struggle to take me down.

A familiar scent distracted me, and I absently allowed my head to turn to follow it. It smelled as if my own version of heaven wafted in.

I stifled a frustrated groan. Did she only bring my favorite of her colognes on this trip? It worked with me, right? Maybe it would work at catching her a new girlfriend.

As if on cue, Sonia strode in, completely put together and ready for the day. Of course she'd already showered and smelled amazing. Wisps of nearly dried and feathered dark hair swept down to lie against perfectly faded sides. Her gray jeans were cuffed at her ankles, revealing tan skin and black slip-on Vans. The first two of the three buttons on her black short-sleeve polo were unbuttoned, the collar down and in place.

She always looked so perfect. And here I sat in my rainbow glasses frames and blood sprayed–looking tie-dyed pants. I suspected that was another aspect she didn't like about me. I could do put together. But that wasn't me in my natural state.

I swore Sonia came out of the womb put together.

My homebody style included sweats and all things comfy. Sometimes I even forgot to put on deodorant.

Okay, more than sometimes.

My going-out style was a little hippie, a little flowy, like last night's dress. Sometimes I sprinkled on a little sexy, also like last night's dress.

I groaned inwardly. Last night.

Pretending to watch the camerapeople, I clocked Michelle waving Sonia over. From the looks of it, Michelle had saved my ex-fiancée a seat.

Sonia put up her hand as if to pass on the offer and found a single chair. She made herself comfortable and started up a conversation with the people nearest her.

Why did Sonia avoid Michelle?

The cameras that were already in place, recording as we all walked into the living room, were readjusted by their operators. I breathed a sigh of relief for the distraction. Additional camerapeople entered and set up their tripods, then pointed to grab shots across the living room, into the entry, and at the front door.

Either Tallia was stopping by to see who was hungover, or…I had no clue. Some talked about the cameras, others quieted and waited. Elise and a couple other producers entered the area from the dining room and stood against the walls, away from the contestants and likely out of camera shot.

Keeping Sonia in my periphery, I nodded along with Sapphire's opinion that dates were starting today. She figured that could be the only reason for all the cameras.

I agreed. And also, I couldn't stop watching Sonia, wondering if she secretly watched me.

Before last night, I thought she no longer loved me. Now I knew better. I also learned last night that along with the love, we held a heavy amount of animosity toward one another.

My therapist mind brushed it off as a necessary aspect in healthy, long-lasting relationships. Having issues wasn't the relationship-breaker people thought. It was the inability to repair those issues that ended relationships.

Severances in relationship bonds happened. It was a part of life. How the two people repaired those breaks was what separated those who went the distance from those who sputtered and crashed.

Growth had to come from somewhere. If two people who loved one another practiced recycling their bullshit into manure together, they could nourish a whole garden. Because reconciliation was the magic elixir of successful romantic connections.

So many times since she dumped me, I wondered what would have happened if I had hung up on her and driven to her house. If I had held her tight, showed her that her fears didn't scare me. Would she have eventually met me halfway if I had been brave enough to begin the reconciliation process before she was able?

I tried to focus on the camerapeople, while a year's worth of thoughts and feelings about Sonia hurdled toward me like a bag of bricks. Sonia, who sat in the same room as me and yet couldn't seem to make eye contact today.

I felt the need to brace for impact, for the next bag of bricks around the corner. Would we talk again? Or did last night confirm for her that by leaving me, she had dodged a bullet?

I used to wonder how we would behave when we first saw one another in public.

Now I knew. And it was uncomfortably comfortable. Like the slow build to the highest part of a roller coaster—at some point, this ride was going to go over the edge and screaming would happen. Last night was just the first hump in the coaster. Did I have it in me to last the whole ride?

When she'd ended things, we were both too tired to fight for it. That was the real reason I didn't drive to her house, and I suspected why she didn't drive to mine.

At the end, screaming didn't happen.

Sighs, giving up. That's what happened.

I watched the camerapeople complete what I had seen enough to know were their last procedures before filming a planned scene.

The villa's great front double doors parted in the center. We leaned forward for a glimpse of what was to come, even a couple on the couch opposite me who would have to wait longer from their vantage point to see whoever was about to enter the villa.

Kamal's lavender slacks hem and bare dark-skinned ankle crossed the threshold first. His leather loafers hovered over the terra-cotta-colored entrance tiles. A handful of people responded with a gasp, two laughs, a few groans.

Mostly groans. Inwardly, I groaned too.

Nothing good tended to come from seeing the show's host, not that I disliked him or anything.

"Hello, hello!" Kamal announced as he walked through the entry. The tile amplified his voice.

More people leaned forward in anticipation. Some gazes stayed fixed on him. Others shifted around the room. I realized I didn't want to get caught on camera watching the expressions of the others and focused my attention back on Kamal.

He was midconversation with a group of contestants, discussing pleasantries. I unconsciously took a sip of my lukewarm tea—lavender and chamomile to help with nerves.

"Well," Kamal said, "as you can guess, I didn't come to discuss omelets and protein shakes." He paused and gave a side-eye to the group he was just talking with. "Would you be mad if I had? Only just come to chat?"

The group laughed and assured him they'd love to have him over for whatever reason.

"Okay, okay," he said, using his hand to brush off that part of the intro as he turned to another camera stationed on a tripod. "I am here on official business." He paused a breath before continuing, "Business of the loving kind."

The room erupted in excitement. Laughter. Clapping. Talking. I observed my fellow contestants as I watched for Sonia's response. She gave a cool grin and a slow nod, like she was game for whatever they were about to throw at her, but not overly excited about any of it.

"It's group date time!" Kamal drew out that last part to emphasize the enormity of the announcement, and it worked.

The intensity in the room went up five notches. Feet excitedly pounded the floor, hands clapped, and squealing happened.

Sonia reached up to scrub the dark tresses atop her head and stopped short. She must have put product in her hair to keep that messy-perfect look and only just remembered.

"In the future," Kamal explained, "you may receive deliveries with invitations for group dates or even one-on-one dates. But for your first one, here's how this works: I am going to announce two separate group dates and two separate one-on-one dates with Tallia. They'll begin tonight. And I've got to say, they're pretty spectacular. She's picked some special things for you. So, let's get to the dates."

Kamal pulled a paper from his back pocket and slowly unfolded it. Sonia leaned forward, her jean-covered knees directly above her perfectly clean shoes. She watched his hands, and I watched her.

"The group dates are as follows," Kamal announced. Some of the names he said made me smile, happy they would get a chance to spend time with Tallia.

"And Sapphire…" Kamal continued.

She gasped.

My focus bounced from Toren to Sapphire as Kamal explained to the group what to expect. She sat up, her hands clutched at her chest, nodding as though he was giving her the information personally.

"You will attend a walking tour through the city of Madrid. Alongside foodie Tallia, learn about Madrid's culinary culture as you sample tapas and wine on this food-focused tour. Visit lively public squares and markets, sample savory tapas and sweet desserts, and taste food from the world's oldest continuously operating restaurant, all with a local guide to lead the way."

Sapphire clapped beside me. LeeAnn, openly staring at Sapphire, did not look happy for my friend. Did she like Sapphire? Had the vibes I was picking up from her for Sapphire last night been right? In a way the vibes looked like they were carrying through to this morning.

Not particularly in a good way. But in a way.

"I love the sound of this date," Sapphire exclaimed, giving two claps and turning to LeeAnn with excitement.

LeeAnn's smile covered the expression she wore seconds ago.

After Kamal quieted the group, he continued, "The second

group date is just as fun and enlightening as the first. The next group of names I call, you will get the chance to take part in a macabre-history-lover's dream. Which Tallia happens to be." He made that last remark with a laugh.

If I wasn't called in this next group, that meant I had a one-on-one with Tallia. The idea terrified me.

I rethought that.

If Sonia wasn't called for this next group, she would be in a one-on-one. She would share a few romantic hours with the beautiful, poised, and kind Tallia. Who didn't drink too much and tell her off.

I hoped Kamal would call Sonia's name. The idea of an awkward date with Sonia and Tallia and three others hurt less than the idea of whatever romantic, private date he was preparing to announce.

"Where we travel today, others have lived their worst nightmares," began Kamal, his voice low like he was introducing a Halloween special. "Walk the horror stories of old Madrid. Spanish Inquisition, terrorism, murders, mysteries, witches, ghosts, and more. Discover the history, and possibly see some of the hauntings, of Madrid."

A mug of tea occupied my left hand, but I crossed the fingers of my right hand and stuck them under my thigh, between the fabric of my pj's and the couch.

"Among those lucky, or unlucky, enough to witness ghosts, are Michelle..." He said a couple more names before I heard the distinct sound of my own name. "And Elly."

Wait? Was he done? Was that it?

Sonia?

My headache pulsated in my right temple.

"Okay. So, you can deduce who the two lucky contestants getting one-on-ones will be," Kamal announced happily. "Before we officially announce them, want to hear where they're going?"

My fellow contestants gave the expected response to continue.

No, *no thank you* to the glimpse into Sonia's night with Tallia. If I could bolt up and out of the room like a flash of lightning, I would have. How far would my body let me push my heart before they both threw in the towel and my brain would have to follow?

"For the first one-on-one, tonight, I've arranged a bit more privacy," Kamal announced. "Those on this date will go for a stroll through El Retiro Park, enjoy a romantic dinner in the Glass Castle, and if things go well, maybe even have nightcaps at a rooftop bar in the heart of the city."

His explanation suggested details that I didn't want to imagine: Long and possibly deep discussions during a stroll in nature, followed by an intimate dinner, probably among old beautiful books, and then nightcaps above the lights and bustle of a romantic and colorful city. I'd watched enough of these types of shows to know at least a kiss would seal the night after such a date.

Contestants swooned.

I worked to keep from retching.

Please don't let that one be Sonia's. Please don't let that one be Sonia's.

"The second one-on-one, tomorrow morning, will be at Casa de Campo, one of the biggest city parks in the world, with plenty of secret places for couples to explore. Those on this date will enjoy a private tour, and then the two of you will retreat to a secluded area for a picnic brunch with cocktails and the area's best seafood tapas," Kamal said, describing the second one-on-one date as though it was just as romantic and unique as the first.

It wasn't. Not by a long shot. The dates were so different, that of the two, I had a preference for Sonia.

I hoped Sonia found happiness. She deserved it. One hundred percent. I wouldn't have been with her if I hadn't thought the world of her. But I didn't want to watch it happen before my eyes, in person, and then again on television along with the rest of the world. No, I was good, thanks. But this was a whole new level of lesbian breakup that I wasn't interested in frontiering. Not a territory I wanted to settle.

"And as you can guess," Kamal went on as my fellow contestants hung from his every word, "your first group date is tomorrow evening. Your second group date is the following evening. And now"—Kamal gave a clap and then rubbed his hands together—"to announce who is going on which one-on-one. The brunch picnic tomorrow at Casa de Campo is…"

It took too long for him to finish.

My gaze bounced to Sonia before I realized I was staring, waiting for any inkling of how she was feeling, hoping for a quick mask drop, to see inside. I couldn't talk to her. I couldn't know her life anymore. I just wanted a peek at the heart I once wrapped my world around.

My need for Sonia had evolved, over the last year, into its own monstrosity. A twisting ache that on the surface could have been satiated by her hug, by inhaling her, hearing her perfect voice while feeling the rumble of her alto transfer from her lips to my ear on her warm breath.

But that was only on the surface, and we all knew the surface held little and hid much. Under that, under the balm that was Sonia, lived miscommunications, injured insecurities, and the repeated perception of rejection. Last night proved that.

Under the balm lived the infectious disease that caused our emergency amputation from one another.

I worked hard to get over her, to heal whatever part of me couldn't let Sonia go. It got to a point when I had to stop talking about her to my friends. Stopped bringing her up in update conversations. I liked it better that way. She went from being the ex I was moving on from to my hidden secret.

I pretended to myself and to others, in hopes it would eventually become my reality.

Fake it till you make it, they said.

Each time I had to drive past her street on the way to visit a client in her neighborhood, my heart raced, tears filled my eyes, and my stomach twisted. I saved those appointment times for the end of the day, so I could rush home to hide afterward.

One sunny day, months ago, I had been driving that route on my way home from seeing a client and drove right past Sonia, her earbuds in, jogging. The thing we used to do together. Even her outfit held painful memories. She wore basketball shorts and a dark tee, an outfit she often worked out in, and one I tried on for laughs, once. I had gotten the laughs, but also an arm looped around my waist pulling me into her, forehead kisses, and compliments on how cute I was in anything and everything.

She didn't appear to notice me the day I passed her jogging on the road, but I noticed her. And seeing her wrecked me.

This morning, she didn't seem to notice me either.

The group clapped in a type of congratulations, and I realized I'd just missed the announcement of the contestant going on the city park date. I made a quick assessment of the faces around me, hoping for a hint of who was chosen.

Shay received pats from the contestants closest to her. Out of everyone, her smile seemed to touch her eyes the most. She must have been chosen.

Which meant...

I closed my mouth and tried to put my tongue where it belonged, glued to the roof of my mouth. A tear escaped and rolled down my cheek. I inhaled and pulled oxygen down to my belly, counting to four before releasing.

I desperately wanted to wipe away evidence of my tear but didn't want to bring attention to myself. I begrudgingly allowed it to snake its way down, leaving a salty trail.

Reminding myself to listen, focus on Kamal's words, helped pull me from the panic spinning a nasty little nest in my abdomen, which currently felt like a hollowed-out tree.

The perfect place for panic to live and grow. Especially after our fight last night.

"And so, this evening's date to El Retiro Park will be the lucky Sonia," Kamal announced, to clapping and congratulations and to my utter dismay.

Charming, beautiful, charismatic Sonia was going on a romantic date in Madrid, Spain tonight. Tonight, Sonia was going to look into Tallia's eyes, see them sparkle, feel a warmth in her own chest, and then lean in to follow those feelings. Tonight, Sonia was going to share her first kiss with Tallia. Probably the first of many in their love story.

A love story I was contractually mandated to watch unfold.

CHAPTER THIRTEEN

Sonia

Engines whisked past, interspersed by honking horns. Twice, I attempted small talk with the driver, and both times produced little more than a smile. I considered pulling a Tony on him, but nervous energy sapped my social pizzazz. Unable to district my thoughts with a conversation, I went back to gazing out the car's back seat window.

To our right stood a row of historical stone buildings, mostly white and cream, lit by the setting sun. To our left stood historical buildings intermixed with contemporary. And in my pocket lived the poem I wrote for Elly, on a folded paper, just in case.

The irony of the poem, connecting our communication issues to traffic on a freeway, was not lost on me as I watched buildings go by, wishing I was here with Elly.

As charming as the city was, I couldn't get this morning out of my mind. Of Elly's many pairs of glasses littering the inside of her bathroom drawer back at home, the rainbow frames were my favorite. I hadn't even fully entered the living room when I saw her, on the couch, cute and comfy in her pj's and glasses.

It only took half a second of spotting her from the tiled entry to almost trip over myself and faceplant into the hard floor. By the time I was in full view of the living room inhabitants this morning, I made sure to not even look in Elly's direction.

Like a photo, the image of Elly in her pj's and glasses sitting, legs folded on the couch, could have been cropped, the background erased, and a new background pasted in place. I couldn't count how many weekend mornings I woke to find her on my couch with Harriet snoring on one side, a steaming mug of coffee on the other, and a book in her lap.

We never lived together, but she had a few drawers and shelves at my place like I had a few at hers. A year and a half ago, I would have never imagined seeing my morning Elly on someone else's couch. This version of her—no makeup, waking up, quiet morning chill—had been one of my favorites. Only I got to see her relaxed, walls down, at-home side, before she started her day, before she was ready to be perceived by others.

I got to see behind it all, where her real magic glimmered and shone.

Now I had to look away while the world got to see.

Since this morning's date's announcement, I tried a couple different times to catch Elly alone. I knew we were each sifting through what happened last night, but I needed her to know I didn't blame her for saying what she said, for how she felt. It didn't feel amazing on my end, but it needed to come out.

Our connection started strong and healthy, grew sick and infected with fear, and then suddenly died. Last night confirmed that Elly and I, our love, still lived, even if just barely. Her purge? Probably the first of many. Removing the pus was an important part of wound care, followed by cleaning, disinfectant, and a bandage, depending on the type of wound.

A conversation, clear and intentional, needed to come next for our connection to heal in any way. If it took a few rounds of purging and cleaning before we could move on to the next steps, I was willing to put in the work. Slap my scrubs on and call me Nurse Sonia.

Unfortunately, sharing a decompression sit-down before I left on a date with Tallia wasn't in the cards for us. And I couldn't stop wondering what she was thinking. Had she been avoiding me earlier? Had last night confirmed for her that she could do better with someone who had their emotional shit together?

This date's timing couldn't have been worse.

On the plus side, plodding forward like a horse with blinders kept me too busy to fully feel the panic climbing my spine like a ladder, tightening each muscle as it ascended.

My car pulled up to the sidewalk to let me out promptly at nine o' clock, from what my silver Citizen watch showed. I had adjusted my watches to the local time when I boarded the flight for Spain. Tonight, I wore my timepiece sporting a green dial because we were going to a park, which inspired my evergreen short-sleeve polo, and I liked to match.

Between the park's black wrought-iron archway and a bustling nighttime street, I stood on a sidewalk lit by decorative streetlights, waiting for Tallia. Branches shifted in the wind created by passing cars. Their shadows exposed and covered my own on the walkway.

In the park, beyond the arch, sat a hill covered with trees and bushes with a pond at its base. A nature oasis in the middle of a city.

Elly and I used to walk Manito Park back home with Harriet in the summer evenings. Breeds like pugs have a rough time with Spokane summers, so they get their walks at night when it's cooler and easier to breathe. During the summer, at night is the best time to visit Manito Park with a lover to avoid other people, stroll slowly, and pause to kiss and take one another in while smelling the roses.

A black sedan, like the one I rode in, slowed to a stop at the sidewalk. I hurried to meet Tallia's car and open the back door. She smiled up at me from the back passenger seat, her brown eyes alight in the twilight.

"Hi," she exclaimed, quickly releasing her buckle to take my hand and stand. She wrapped her arms around my shoulders in an embrace.

"May I?" I offered my arm.

She tucked her arm in mine, and we walked toward the arch.

A cameraman walked backward with ease, in front of us, as he filmed us entering the park.

"So, what are you most looking forward to tonight?" Tallia asked as we meandered the cement path toward a woman waiting beside two camera operators. The rhinestones on the shoulders of her fitted dark blazer sparkled under the lamplight whenever we passed one. Her skinny dark slacks and heels pulled it all together.

We reached the woman as she offered her hand to shake ours. "Hello. My name is Isabella, and I will be your tour guide this evening." She wore a loose, silky white sleeveless blouse and gray dress slacks. Her straight black hair was tied back a low ponytail.

"Hola, thank you so much for having us," Tallia said, excitement dripping from the uptick of her voice.

"It is my pleasure," Isabella answered and began the tour. As we walked the path, she opened her arms in front of her as though gesturing to everything before us. "Welcome to El Retiro Park, the lungs of the city of Madrid."

Trees and bushes cast shadows looming ahead and over us. Lamps lit our path as the sun lay on the horizon, its light covered by city buildings. To our left stood lightposts surrounded by hedges, and the city beyond the wrought-iron fence. To our right, benches bordered the edge of the path, where cement met curb and a vast blanket of rolling grass dotted by bushy topped trees. A half moon hung low in the sky waiting its turn to lengthen shadows with its silky gleam.

Tallia and I kept in stride with Isabella, the bacheloress's arm still linked to mine.

Isabella walked in front of us and to the left, narrating facts about the park as we walked. Tallia and I barely kept our eyes on Isabella and only seemed to bounce our attention to her the first few words of each new statement before another aspect of the park caught our attention.

Twilight sky melted new shades of pink and orange across the heavens like bright watercolor paints spilled onto a darkening azure backdrop. Darkness dripped onto nature's grass, trees, and bushes until they donned regal evening cloaks to tuck the day into night.

"I am currently leading you to the Great Pond, the Estanque Grande," Isabella said, midstride. "After the pond we will complete tonight's tour at Palacio de Cristal, the Glass Palace, where a romantic dinner will be waiting for you two to dine amidst Spain's world-renowned art."

Tallia flexed her arm to squeeze mine when Isabella mentioned dinner, and I figured she'd also had a meal delivered to her place an hour before our cars picked us up for our date.

Preparing for tonight's one-on-one involved more than an outfit change and hair restyling. It included a long meeting with Elise, filming a predate interview, and being ready to go an hour early so I could eat alone in my room. No one wanted to watch people eat and try to carry a conversation at the same time, so most dating show segments filmed over a candlelight dinner did not include actual eating.

❖

Tallia sat across from me at a circular wrought-iron table. Despite the walls of glass, the darkness outside made the space inside feel quaint and peaceful. Candles, long and lean, flickered as our table's centerpiece. The dancing orangish-red glow created a light show, reflected in the rhinestones on her blazer.

"I know I already said it, but I want to tell you again." Tallia rested her hands on the table to hold mine. "I appreciate your honesty tonight, on the boat."

I wanted to shrink under the reminder but gave a confident smile and nod. Maybe it was the illusion of privacy that caused me to open up, as I paddled the little boat over tranquil water in the twilight evening hours. I told her about losing my dad, how at first my mom and I clung to one another for comfort. But things were changing and settling into a new normal without him.

"It's important to me that I be my authentic self," I repeated from earlier tonight. "If I can't show up as me, I don't see the point in showing up."

"Which is why I chose you for my initial one-on-one," she quickly responded. "We're on a dating reality show that hypes the fantasy aspect. And not just the falling-in-love-on-vacation kind of fantasy, but the pursuing-self-growth-alongside-your-partner type of fantasy. It's like a facade, a social media post on steroids."

Tallia gestured to everything around us. We were situated in a gorgeous glass castle of a greenhouse that had been turned into an art museum on the water. Candles flickered not just in the center of our table, but in clusters, varying in height and number, placed expertly to illuminate paintings and plants. To cast shadows on the rest, hinting to us and maybe eventual viewers of the existence of hidden corners and darkened spaces behind huge pots of cascading vine plants.

"Any ounce of realness I can get, I'll take it," she added.

"I'm not here for a fantasy," I said, pointing to the facade of dinner sitting in front of us. "I want real." As per the producer's request before filming our dinner scene, we were each allowed to take one bite, and no more. Both dishes of seafood paella were props, deliciously authentic meals we were not allowed to eat.

"Me too. A love that'll last long after filming." She leaned back into her chair and exhaled. "Which is why I have to bring up the elephant in the room."

Her shift in tone and body language threw me, but I didn't show as much.

"You're an ex to an original contestant," she stated. "But I haven't seen you together with anyone here. In fact, I've got theories on every ex but you, so I'm wondering if it's safe to say you two are done."

I almost choked on my own breath. I coughed on an awkward laugh, racking my brain for a response. Elly and I failed at ending last night on the same page about moving forward on the show. My preference was to keep my focus on Elly, whether we left Europe as friends or together. More than any person here, I wanted to invest my time in Elly.

"To be honest, I don't know how to answer that," I said. "Because you're right, we haven't been able to discuss it, and I'd feel bad speaking for her without her consent."

A smile lifted the edges of her mouth. "I think that's honorable."

I shrugged. "Or cowardice." So far, only Katy and Heather claimed one another at the villa, happy to be there with a close friend. Tallia may have had her theories, but only one couple confirmed them. "We didn't end very well. It was during my life implosion, after my dad died. I was consumed with grief and questioned everything, including her. I did a shit job of breaking up with her."

"It makes a lot of sense, though," she said, scooting her chair back away from the table. "Huge life changes have a way of putting couples to the fire and exposing their weaknesses. I think it's indicative of how they'll show up for you later. Looks like your ex failed the test."

I pushed my chair back and considered Tallia's opinion. "I don't know about that. I think we failed each other."

"See? That's what I'm talking about. You have every right to be angry at her and you're not." Tallia stood and offered her hand to me. I grasped it and stood. "I heard there's a rooftop nearby with Disney cocktails waiting for us, if you're ready to go."

I let her lead us out. "Wait. Disney cocktails? Kamal didn't mention they'd be Disney themed." I pretended to shake my head in self-admonishment. "Here I was going to order you a lemon drop, and now I find out you'd prefer a Princess Peach."

Tallia laughed. I opened the glass and iron door, taking us from inside to outside. A light breeze danced along the night air. The two mobile camera operators followed.

"Actually…" she said, as we made our way back along the trail from where we came. The moon stretched shadows across dark knolls and stone sculptures. "Princess Peach would probably get the bar in trouble, seeing as Disney and Nintendo are two separate companies."

I gave an amused laugh as we turned a corner on the lamp-lit path and the arched entrance we came through earlier showed itself. "So, tell me about your undercover interest in law."

Tallia belted out a laugh. "Undercover interest."

We neared the stationary camera setup where a producer and cameraperson talked. They paused their discussion, and the little red light on the professional camcorder came to life, catching us walking the dark park, hand in hand, laughing.

I pulled my hand away from Tallia's. She shot me a questioning look before walking ahead to meet the producer.

After our middate interviews in the park, we made our way

to the waiting black sedan parked where we arrived, taking in the lights and sounds of lively Madrid, under the cool kiss of the moon.

I gestured for Tallia to get in before me, and then once she was in place I scooted myself into the back of the car. The driver pulled our vehicle onto the streets of late-night Madrid. The lack of a cameraperson gave our cocoon a uniquely private feel, despite the little cameras installed throughout the car.

"Why'd you pull away from me back there?" Tallia asked. "Completely dropped my hand like your ex just walked up or something."

"I'm sorry about that," I said, trying to gauge how far she wanted to go into the topic.

When I noticed the producer and the stationary cameras, all ready to ask about our romantic feelings for one another, I panicked.

Already this felt like a chore, keeping me from Elly. But I came here for an experience and didn't want to regret shortchanging myself, missing out on the sights of Madrid, to get tied up in hashing things out with my ex.

Which was unfair to Tallia.

"Sorry about rejecting me or sorry you came?" she asked, cocking her head, as though she dared me to pick one.

"Not rejection," I corrected, "panic." And then I wondered if I had just made it worse in her mind.

"You deserve to have a good time, not worry about your ex," she answered, softer. After a breath of silence, she changed the subject. "Why are you single? I mean, you're hot, smart, and charming. I'm curious, what gives?"

"Oh," I stammered, mentally searching the crevices of my brain for a response and failing miserably. "I mean…"

I had tried to find love after Elly. I didn't blanket Spokane's queer scene with my prowess or anything, but I gave it a good try. When I joined my friends for a night out at our favorite watering hole, and they urged me to make small talk with a woman, I didn't shy away from it. When they brought along their single sapphic friends, I did the whole flirting in earnest thing.

Every time, we either ran out of things to talk about or I quickly surmised she wouldn't be a good fit. When Elly entered my life, holy shit did she take me by storm. Elly Straus was all lightning and thunder, and everything deep and adventurous. Storm Elly. The most breathtaking and elusive storm you could encounter.

It was possible I had been looking for a storm of a woman to sweep me off my feet again. Maybe I hoped if I found another, I could try again and do it right. I doubted lightning would strike twice for me, though.

"Can I tell you my thoughts?" Tallia asked, like she hadn't already been freely sharing.

"Please do," I said, thankful for the break from trying to understand myself enough to put it all into words.

Tallia placed her hand on top of mine on my thigh and looked into my eyes. "It's hard to hear negative truths about your ex from an unbiased outside view."

I hardly thought Tallia was unbiased, but I let her continue.

"Trust me, I know," she continued. "But oftentimes the outsider can see things you can't."

"I won't disagree with that," I said, uncomfortable by Tallia's intensity, but unsure what to do about it.

Tallia leaned in, her hand heavy on mine as she pressed a peck of a kiss to my lips. I sat frozen, my eyes open.

"I'm glad we're on the same page." She pulled away after only a short moment and flashed a smile that told me she didn't notice my lack of enthusiasm. "I have something to give you."

I used the pause to internally regroup. The kiss caught me off guard, but I mentally prepared to stop it if she tried again.

She turned and pulled a clear plastic box from the empty front passenger seat. In seconds I realized the contents—a bundle of three violet plants, tied together with purple ribbon. Panic returned with a vengeance, thudding my pulse in my ear.

"Sonia," Tallia said with a flirtatiously warm smile, "I had a wonderful time with you tonight. I'd like to get to know you more. Will you accept these violets?"

She opened the plastic container and held out the sweet-smelling bundle. Of the reality dating shows I consumed, none included rejecting the offered rose, or in my case, violets. Kamal never mentioned how accepting violets would affect the exes on the show. With no alternative responses to think of, I accepted the purple flowers.

"I am so glad you had such a great time," I said, clutching the stems in my fist and wondering what the hell that meant for Elly and me on the show. "Thank you."

She exhaled and smiled. "Okay, now that that's done"—she shook out her hands and released a tense laugh—"I'm ready for drinks harder than wine."

Glad for the topic change, I said, "Those were your first date violets, weren't they?"

She smiled and gave a sheepish nod. "I was terrified."

I laughed. "You shouldn't have been. Anyone would be stupid to turn you down. You're the whole package." And she deserved to have someone beside her in the back seat of the car, during a one-on-one, who melted at the thought of being hers.

Her smile dropped and she tilted her head slightly, eyeing me with the look that so far tonight ended with an opinion of hers.

She sat up straight to look out the windshield. "I needed this, tonight. Thank you."

She closed her eyes and seemed to melt into the moment, adding to my growing guilt that I was allowing her to invest time in me when I wished I was with Elly.

"Good," I said. "The villa is twenty-four-seven tension. You deserve to get away and think."

"You're right, I thought a lot tonight," she responded, the eyeshadow sparking on her lids as streetlights passed. "And after tonight I'll have even more to think about."

"Oh?" I asked, more to keep the conversation flowing than anything else.

"I like you," she said, opening her eyes to lock her gaze onto mine. "This contest isn't as easy as everyone vying for one. The bacheloress has to employ game strategy too, in this one."

"What kind of strategy?" I asked, increasingly thankful Elly and I kept our connection private at the villa.

In an instant, Tallia leaned in, gently traced an index finger from my temple to my jaw, and tried to plant a kiss.

Before our lips touched, after she closed her eyes, I pulled away.

Her eyes snapped open and her jaw set.

Tallia cleared her throat, sat up straight, and repositioned herself in her seat, as far away from me as possible.

Pop music murmured from the back speakers, too quietly to hear lyrics. Streetlights lit the leather interior for a moment before we descended back into darkness. Tires rolled rhythmically across pavement.

I waited for Tallia to take the lead on what was best for her, despite wanting to overexplain myself. I couldn't conjure romantic feelings for someone when I still had a chance with Elly.

Seeing Elly after a year apart was like taking a defibrillator to the heart. All the chaos inside, the questions erratically knocking into themselves, were jolted when Elly looked at me. With her, the rhythm of life flowed best.

But how could I tell Tallia? Because she didn't deserve to be caught in the middle either. And if I did offer more clear responses to how I felt, how would it affect Elly? I refused to risk fracturing the shaky ground she and I stood on.

Tallia exhaled and cleared her throat. "I'm so sorry, but I need to change our plans this evening," she said to the driver. "We won't be going out. Please take us back to the villa."

Chapter Fourteen

Elly

All day, I watched the clocks. The digital microwave numbers, the huge analog hanging in the living room, the alarm beside my bed, even the outdoor thermostat combo hiding in the trellis shade of the pool patio.

I could not, would not, be anywhere near the front door when Sonia descended the stairs looking and smelling like the hottest lesbian in the world. Seeing Sonia excited and ready for a date with another woman would break me.

I had already gone through this once.

When she broke up with me, I secretly feared it had been for another woman. I spent weeks emotionally bracing for the gossip to trickle down to me from well-meaning acquaintances.

After that belief faded, another brought sleepless Saturday nights envisioning Sonia dancing at Kitty's with a new woman. Dabbing soft kisses on the woman's neck, whispering naughty promises for later, as they swayed to the beat. I imagined from the woman's view, seeing Sonia approach her, want and lust and love for the woman entwined in her gaze.

Since breaking up, I avoided Sonia's favorite spots for one core reason: I couldn't witness seeing her love for me shown to another. When she offered to get Tallia a drink last night, my inner panic meter hit the yellow warning section. It was dangerously close to forcing me to witness the thing I just couldn't.

I planned to hang tight in my room from about thirty minutes before Kamal said Sonia needed to leave, to around thirty minutes after. Just in case she was early or late. Not that I had ever seen her late to anything. But when eight, then eight thirty rolled around, I figured I was safe.

Now I kept an eye on the clock in the pool canopy area, counting the hours of their date. Sapphire had been right, the sun's warmth felt more palatable at night. It seemed every passing thirty-minute chunk Sonia spent with Tallia, my fear of losing her ratcheted tighter.

"You heading in soon?" Sapphire asked, standing above where I lay on a foldable lounge. She wore a baby-blue pleated skirt, matching heels with white puffy pom-poms on the toes, and a white crop top. Her light hair hung past her shoulders from two ponytails. "I've already gotten ready, come back down, and you're still out here."

Twinkle lights wrapped around tree trunks and sparkled behind branches. The steady thrum of the pool's filtration system joined the cadence of leaves dancing in the breeze.

"First," I said, "how do your outfits keep getting cuter and cuter?"

Sapphire responded with a curtsy.

"And also, do you think there's rules against sleeping out here?" I asked.

"Only if you're drunk enough to make it worth their while," she promptly, and probably accurately, responded.

"Drama?" I pretended to ask seriously.

She caught on to my sarcasm and played along. "It would appear so." She made a show of placing her hands on her hips and taking in the panoramic view of the pool patio. "Get your butt to the karaoke party with me, take a few shots, find some drama, and pretend to pass out here. You'll be golden."

I groaned. "I forgot about the karaoke party." I was busy avoiding my ex. I sat up and swung my legs to the side of the lounge to stand.

"That's the spirit," Sapphire joked.

I hoisted myself up.

"Beauty *and* grace," she quipped.

I fanned her away with my hand, not a drop of alcohol in my system, yet drunk on postpanic sleepiness. "Ugh," I added for emphasis.

Sapphire playfully scoffed. "Your excitement is almost uncontainable. Almost."

I stopped moping and stood up straight. I doubted she meant it as a warning, but that's how I took her statement. Because if *she* noticed, who *else* clocked my lack of luster for making connections here?

When it came to dating shows like this one, everyone kissed on one-on-one dates, as long as the mood was right. And I knew Sonia. She had a charm about her, a way of crafting the right vibe when she wanted. She also had a way of making a girl's knees melt when she quieted her gravelly voice and placed her words securely in your ear for only you to hear.

Gave me tingles just thinking about it.

Which was the opposite of comforting.

"All right," I said, grabbing my towel and book from the lounge. What was I doing forcing the clock to move slower by watching it? "Let me run upstairs and freshen up, and I'll meet you in the game room."

Sapphire gave a little clap-jump with a squee.

"By the way," I said, circling back to make sure the compliment hit as genuine, "your outfit is hot. I hope for your sake, if your ex is here, they're eating their heart out."

I looked her up and down while she smiled and gave a cocky head tilt. If she did have an ex at the villa, she was unfazed.

"Thanks." She curtsied again. "I'm going for queer Britney. She was my idol growing up. *Guarantee* I'll be singing at least one of hers tonight."

I pretended to sear my index finger touching her bare forearm and pulled back.

"What did you bring to wear?" Sapphire asked as I turned to go in and she walked with me.

"I'm not creative or smart enough to bring an outfit matching my chosen karaoke song," I answered without answering.

On our preparation document, we had to list at least two karaoke songs we wanted to sing. I figured they were filling their songs queue for the house in preparation. I wrote down three songs, not sure which mood I would be feeling when the time came to sing it. One: "Leader of the Pack" by The Shangri-Las, an oldies song I used to sing with my parents. Two: "Slumber Party" by Ashnikko and Princess Nokia, because sapphic dating show. And three: Sonia's and my unspoken, no-questions-asked song, "If the World Was Ending" by Saxe and Julia Michaels.

At the time, I thought it was smart. I thought if she watched the show, she'd see it and decide I was sweet for thinking of her. Though now, as I walked to my room to get ready for an all-sapphic karaoke party featuring alcohol, anxiety, and questionable decisions, the truth struck me as yet another ironic piece of this shit pie.

I laughed to myself.

"What's funny?" Sapphire asked, ready to part ways with me as I headed to the entry and she to the game room.

Well, I wanted to say, *I'm going to sing our get-back-together song to a room full of single sapphics while my ex is on a date.* More like funny in the pathetic way.

I paused on the first step, wrapping my hands around the wooden banister and allowing my weight to lean on it. "I'm going to sing 'If the World Was Ending' by Saxe and Julia Michaels." I let go of the rail and hopped up a step. "And I think I'll wear a miniskirt too. Black. Very Julia Michaels."

"There you go!" Sapphire sang. "Now she's getting in the game."

I flashed a smile and ran up the stairs.

Not even thirty minutes later I emerged from my room a new woman, sporting a short backed dull-sequined skirt, all black high-top Converse, and a scoop-neck black band T-shirt. When the show prep paperwork listed a karaoke party as an event to pack for, I knew I wanted to bring an elevated version of my karaoke outfit.

And yes, I had a karaoke outfit.

I looked it over in the full-body mirror standing beside the balcony door. Moonlight barely lit the villa's grounds in the distance, past the illuminated front fountain and driveway. The dark night and I wore a similar mood, edgy in a way that promised adventure.

I spun to check my butt and gave a nod of approval.

My normal summer karaoke outfit consisted of jean shorts, any old Converse, and any clean band T-shirt. My friends joked that karaoke Elly was not the same person as normal Elly. I couldn't put my finger on why the idea of belting my heart out made me want to don tight shorts and skirts instead of my usual long flowy ones. Maybe the outfit offered me an alter ego I needed to embrace for bravery. I was no songbird. Singing in front of strangers, or anyone, felt more personal than I liked, when I didn't have the vocal cords to fall back on.

I skipped down the stairs with a confidence my karaoke alter ego knew well.

The game room proved easy to find in the sprawling villa. It helped that a popular Celine Dion song led the way. After crossing through open double doors, I entered what looked like a hybrid between an old-world study and a large lounge. People played air hockey, pool, and darts. A bartender blended the contents of a shaker, the bar in front of him scattered with open wine variations, and the shelf behind him full of alcohol and mixer selections.

I made my way to the leather sectional facing the end wall at the far corner of the room. Words scrolled across the wall-mounted TV as a fellow contestant sang a song I couldn't place.

Beth, the firefighter who gave Tallia a replica hat on the first night, faced the TV as they sang. Their raspy voice matched the cadence of the song perfectly. When they turned away from the screen for a second, their face looked serious, almost stricken, expressing a sadness the song's words only attempted.

My heart hurt for them. I knew that pain.

They sang pleading words to the lost love of the song. Beth's free hand drew one side of a woman's figure in the air.

I smoothed the glamorized version of my karaoke skirt as I stood behind the sectional, feeling my body sway with the tune. The song sounded so familiar, as though the notes twined around my heart and squeezed. Tears filled my eyes, and I smiled at the type of painful pleasure music had the unique power to inflict.

I remembered the artist's name, Dermot Kennedy.

Beth bent down to their right side, like the heaviness of heartache took its toll. They belted out the ending on a melodic question, asking how they were letting all their love go.

Beth dropped to their knees, closed their eyes, and bowed their head.

Their audience on the couch sprang to their feet, clapping and cheering. Beth took a second to find their composure and pull themself up from the ground, lifting their head and fixing their sorrow into a smile.

"Everyone experiences suffering." Sonia used to quote her dad, even after he died. "True and genuine love makes the suffering worth it, because no matter what, love is the light at the end of the tunnel."

In the months after we broke up, I wondered what her dad would have thought about the way we ended. He had always been so supportive of us as a couple, of our love. And I wished I had asked him when I had the chance, what if it's the love that causes the suffering? What then?

After Beth left the spot between the couch and the TV, our temporary stage, Katy looked to the group on the couch. "Anyone want to go next?"

No one raised their hand or spoke up. They only shook their heads.

"You're good to go," she told Sapphire.

"Oh, uh…" Sapphire turned to look to the open doors leading to the rest of the house. "I need a hot tea before doing a Britney. I don't have her pipes."

"Fair, fair," Katy said. "For Britney, I'll wait patiently."

Sapphire left the game room for the kitchen.

"Elly, what about you?" Katy asked. "Wanna sing?"

I gave a nod. I could contribute to this evening's release of emotions through poetic words to melody. A little tension release would do me good. "Can you pull up my songs and play 'If the World Was Ending' by Saxe and Julia Michaels?"

"Sure."

Katy handed me the mic and went to work.

The familiar piano tune started slowly. I took a breath and began to sing.

The words' sharp sting pricked my heart. A year. I remembered when I first sang this, thinking of Sonia. How the idea of a year without her seemed like some sort of torturous hell. A hell I could now say I had lived through. At least there was that.

Except I hadn't figured out how to keep it from ripping my heart out. Even after a year.

I sang about knowing we weren't right for one another, past a growing lump in my throat.

Tears filled my eyes.

I let them.

Emotions rode upon melody as I sang of a single moment when our incompatibilities and fears didn't have to matter anymore and we could just be together.

I looked up to my audience. They watched, transfixed. Maybe it was the outfit. Maybe it was the song, or Beth's courage. But I allowed my longing for Sonia to drip from my lowered voice, while tears wound down my cheeks.

Sapphire sat with mug in hand, her brows knit together as though she felt my hurt. I gave her a soft half smile before returning my gaze to a flowery design on the rug beneath my feet.

Pulling an inhale deep into my belly, I closed my eyes to truly feel the instrumental notes before belting out the last line. I didn't have to *try* to fill each word with inflection. I wore the last lines as though I plucked a dress from a wardrobe deep within my soul and slipped it over my shoulders. The pattern adorning the gown? My pleadings to feel Sonia again, to be swept up in the bubble of our own love where our differences didn't matter.

Ready to deliver the final emotional blow, I lifted my eyes to promise that if ever there came a time when we were free to cast our issues aside and love one another, I would be there.

Sonia stood behind the couch, still, watching, looking perfect.

My breath hitched, shattering my attempt to finish strong. My voice cracked on the last line. Piano notes softly played the song away as I stared like a deer in oncoming headlights.

My audience gave a standing ovation.

Still, all I saw was Sonia, her glassy stare locked onto me, as the only person in the villa who *knew* my cry.

I tossed the mic to Sapphire, who had just set her mug of tea on a side table.

"I'll have to catch your next one." I barely got the last word out before tears sprang from their enclosures. I bolted from the room, through the kitchen and living room and entry, up the stairs to my room.

So much for my karaoke outfit and my badass alter ego. When Sonia was around, all I could be was me. Needy, sad, trembling me.

CHAPTER FIFTEEN

Sonia

"Sonia's back!" someone yelled when the group turned to watch Elly flee from the game room and noticed me standing behind them.

Walking in on Elly holding a mic while sporting a band T-shirt brought back memories. The skirt, though, accentuating her sexy calf muscle lines above high-tops, was a new addition. I was a fan.

"How'd it go?"

"What's Tallia like?"

"What did you talk about?"

"Did you kiss?"

Questions rained down like an invasion, as my fellow contestants left their pool game, walked around the couch from karaoke, or just stayed in place and stared intently.

Michelle took the lead, navigating the furniture in a hurry to offer a hug. Hesitant from Tallia's kiss in the car, I stepped back.

She gasped. "You got the first one-on-one violets."

The huge game room quieted.

Shit.

I'd arrived home and heard Elly echoing through the house. My plan to hide the bundle of violets in my bedroom before hitting the confession room and then joining the others fell out of my mind when her voice filled it.

Technically, yes, Tallia did give me a violet bundle. Before I awkwardly avoided her kiss. Before she abruptly ended the date and all but booted me from her car. Violets or not, Tallia wasn't going to keep me around.

Within minutes of transferring to my own car to be taken back to the villa, Elise called. "They're saying she's pissed," Elise warned through the sedan's speakers. "And she won't say why. What happened? From all the updates I was getting, things were going beautifully."

I massaged the base of my neck in the back seat, not sure how to answer Elise's question.

"I don't know," was all I could think to say. If Tallia didn't want to share, why would I? They'd figure it out soon from the cameras in the car, anyway.

"At least you have violets to keep you safe at the next ceremony. This could go either way, though."

Despite Tallia's anger, I didn't regret my decision to pass on her offered kiss. The last time I made out in the back of a car, Elly and I were in an Uber coming home from Kitty's on Pride night. She had been more than tipsy, like last night. But this was before the problems, before my dad died, before my world fell apart leaving me to question reality. To question Elly.

Elly's pre-villa version of more-than-tipsy started with the cutest one-liners that made no sense, and ended in the dark with what we jokingly called Succubus Elly. No part of me felt the need to risk my shot at experiencing Elly's version again, over Tallia's.

"Okay, well. Wait, hold on." Elise was speaking to someone else, but I couldn't understand what she said. After a muffled shuffle, she spoke again, this time to me. "Okay, when you get back to the house, we need your first stop to be the confession room."

I groaned.

"You still there?" Elise asked after moments of silence from my end.

"Yeah," I answered.

"Okay, I'll find you when you get back to the house. But before I do, confession, okay?"

"Got it," I said before she hung up.

Except I never made it to the confession room. I didn't have the opportunity.

From the moment I entered the villa, Elly's apocalyptic song for us crawled like fingers upon musical notes to find me, snatch me up, and draw me in. Succubus Elly's siren song. Desperate words spoken to a slow melody called for my heart from the familiar voice of my lost love. My chest ached in response.

Six months into our relationship, maybe seven, she had just finished reading a novel about the end of the world. She had been lying on my couch when she closed the book, sighed, and pronounced that book to be the best book she ever read. With Elly, the last book she loved was the best book she ever read.

I remembered it had been close to the time the sun went down because of the way the sheer orange of my curtains made her glow like fire. Especially when she talked passionately about books. She shut the cover, looked at me where I stood in the kitchen, and declared, "We need an apocalypse song."

I had been finishing making food for Harriet. Elly hadn't gotten Rowdy yet. Harriet jumped from Elly to the opposite armrest, waiting for me to set her bowl down.

"You're going to need to be more specific," I said, laughing.

With Elly, she could have been talking about wanting to find songs about apocalypses, or wanting to have an official apocalypse anthem to play the world out with.

"Like a Bat-Signal," she answered.

"Oh." I finished mixing Harriet's food and moved to place her bowl on the mat in the kitchen. She jumped from the couch to chow down, and I took her place beside Elly. "So, like, a way to call the end of the world?" I wiped my hands on the kitchen towel I held.

"The story I read was about the end of the world, but like, politically. A new way of living takes hold and changes the everyday landscape for societies. The main character is a top scholar on this super difficult technology, and she's only this proficient because she had to give up a relationship to dedicate her life to learning it. Both her and her girlfriend agreed to part ways because they both had bigger roles to play in the grand scheme of things. And they do in the story. Her girlfriend ends up leading a tactical unit in the revolution."

"That's beautiful," I said. "And incredibly sad."

"It's a phenomenal book," Elly said. "But when they parted ways, they agreed on a song to play that meant they were going to meet at a certain spot and die together. Because they would work for the good of everyone until it was time to die. Then they'd be able to be together."

"Damn, that sounds depressing," I said. "Why music, though? If it's the end of the world?"

"Because in the story, hand crank radios are the only communication left. And a song reveals very little, but says so much. So that's how people end up communicating," Elly answered. "By singing songs over radio waves."

Now I stood in a villa game room in Spain, at the end of a rough night, having just heard the last line of Elly's apocalyptic song to me. Her cry to feel me, hold me one last time. And fuck if my body didn't ache in response. Didn't call back, inwardly begging her to hear my reply.

"What was she wearing?" Beth asked, probably my favorite person in this house. Out of everyone, Beth seemed the most genuine. I thought of them as a house buddy.

I snapped out of my thoughts. "A black suit with rhinestones," I answered.

"Of course." Beth gave a nod and sipped their drink.

"I forgot, I have to go do an after-date confessional," I said on my way out of the game room.

Sounds of disappointment, including a couple boos, trailed me as I headed to the kitchen. But I didn't care. They wanted gossip, and I wanted Elly. They could wait.

I jogged upstairs to Elly's room, knocked, paced in front of the room, and knocked again. When she didn't answer, I cracked the door and whispered her name. Her bedroom was empty. If she didn't head here, or the living room...Ah.

Elly liked to be outside when she was upset.

After a quick check for her in the confessional room, I cut

through the living room for the pool patio. Two contestants giggled in the hot tub. Neither was Elly. I considered checking the garden patio where I first saw her, during the brunch. But I doubted the spot held positive significance to her. There was a little side garden Beth showed me that made me think of Elly. My group of exes had shuffled through it on our way to the garden patio for the brunch.

From the patio, I walked across the grass and took a stone path that continued on under a gate. I pressed the iron latch and swung the gate forward, giving way to a large rectangular patch of mulch, stones, and various plants, from flowering bushes to flower patches.

Faint sobs added a discernably audible layer to the nighttime echoes of crickets and frogs. Rounding the corner on the path, I found Elly sitting on a stone bench in an alcove made of tall shrubs.

"I don't want you to see me like this," Elly whined, not looking up.

A solar-powered garden light, staked into the ground, pointed its soft glow at a lavender plant feet away. Her ponytail cascaded down her shadowed forehead and face, revealing her undercut. Lotus fit her.

"Like what?" I asked. "Gorgeous and sad?"

"Ha," she said woefully. "Demoted from deep, adventurous Storm Elly to gorgeous, sad Just Elly."

So, she remembered Storm Elly, one of my officially unofficial titles for her. I had a handful of them, collected in those random moments she did or said something that made my heart want to burst with adoration and love for her.

The fact that I had created so many titles in the two years we were together should have already occurred to me.

"No one is being demoted," I assured her. "Is there room on that bench for one more?"

She exhaled and scooted over. I took up the empty space on the short bench and started to rub her back but thought better and returned my hands to my lap.

Since our argument last night, I had tried to talk to her, repeatedly, and she avoided me. Why would she all of a sudden want me to touch her, directly after a date with another woman?

"Did you mean to sing our apocalypse song?" I asked, because since walking into the house I needed to know.

"I didn't think you'd hear me," she uttered. "I'm mortified. You weren't supposed to hear that."

A sharp pain cracked through my chest. "So then, you don't see a future for us?" When I heard her sing that song, the memory of her explaining the idea flooded me, and more than anything I wanted to pick up where we left off.

I wanted more songs with Elly, more stories and memories, kisses and jokes and officially unofficial titles. I wanted random end-of-the-world ideas on Tuesday evenings, and jokes that made no sense on Saturday mornings over coffee.

"What future, Sonia?" she asked on a shaky, tear-filled voice. "We can't even talk about the past."

"What do you want to talk about?" I asked, desperate to know what I had to do to get back our karaoke nights with friends, when our constant embrace only broke to sing or clap.

"I want to talk about…" Elly exhaled a sigh and raised her head to meet my eyes. "I want to talk about why, when your world was crumbling, did you turn away from me instead of toward me? Why did you assume the worst of me, when I had never before done what you accused me of?" New tears sparkled and spilled over, tracing new paths among the previous ones. "How, when you love someone so much you want to spend your life with them, can you so easily end what you have with them over a phone call? A fucking phone call, Sonia."

I had no helpful response. All I could do was listen, let her get out what I should have afforded her a year ago.

Tears poured as she worked to catch her shaking breath. Through quivering lips, she continued, "You couldn't have waited to get more information because you loved me so much and intended to keep loving me? Or asked me to drive over and hold you and reassure you without talking? Because I would have fucking done that. In a heartbeat, I would have done that. I knew you were struggling, and I love you! I wanted to be there for you, but you pushed me away, afraid to tell me the real shit you were struggling with, so you blamed me and cut me out."

Elly inhaled deeply. Her exhale was smoother, less ragged. She kept going. "Or maybe you didn't know you were struggling with deeper shit because of everything going on. Also valid. It's not like I don't have practice sifting through my own shit. I'd have helped you process your thoughts like a best friend, because we were that too. You didn't just rip my fiancée from me in the matter of a simple phone call. You tore from me my *very best friend*. And I get that you were grieving, God, I do, as much as I can, I do. But we promised we would slay our own dragons to be together, Sonia Comstock."

I listened, trying not to inwardly assign a response to everything she said but rather to hear her.

Her shoulders dropped on her exhale. She relaxed enough to look around, to see more than red. She eyed the bundle of violets that draped sadly from my left hand at the edge of the cement bench. I had forgotten about those.

Her shoulders climbed higher as she closed her eyes and shook her head. "Your date went well, I see," she said.

Shit.

"I planned to tell you about tonight, I was just letting you vent, get it out," I said.

As though she was pulling on a mask she would typically wear for a stranger, she coughed on an exhale and stood. She began to walk the path, away from me and toward the gate, but stopped. "I don't want to assume," she said. "But I also don't have it in me to hear certain stuff right now." She huffed out a breath. "Do you mind if I ask a couple questions, get simple answers, and then process so we can delve deeper later?"

"Of course," I said, reaching out for her hand and not getting a response.

"Thank you," she said, emotionless. "I want to talk to you tonight, still. I know it's late, but I want us to try to at least be on the same page around here before another day goes by. Before another announcement out of left field."

I nodded, happy to know where her mind was at, hoping our talk tonight would be sooner than later.

"First," she said with a semismile, "was dinner amazing?"

"They didn't let us have more than a bite," I answered. "But I sneaked an extra on our way out, and yes, you would have loved the seafood paella." I thought about you the whole time, not just in how you reminded me of saffron, or how gorgeous your skin would have looked in the candlelight's glow while we steamed the glass walls.

She offered a nod. "Good, I'm glad. Was it a romantic night?"

I genuinely scoffed. "No, it wasn't."

Her smile grew, and it looked to me like she stood a little taller too.

"Did you kiss?" she asked. A simple, easy question.

I swallowed, racking my mind for a simple answer other than the only one coming up. "Yes."

She turned abruptly.

"Wait." I stood to grab her hand, but she kept walking toward the gate.

Her pace quickened and I didn't know if I should chase her or let her cool off.

"It only happened once!" I called as she ran to the gate and allowed it to slam behind her.

When two broken pieces of a heart found one another and collected the needle and thread to painfully resew the bond they'd lost, the weight of one misstep was enough to burst those new stitches and leave the two halves worse off for trying.

Chapter Sixteen

Elly

In a whirlwind of emotion, I snatched the shower caddy from the edge of my dresser and spun on my Converse to lunge for my pj's on my bed. No actual thoughts cleared themselves enough to be known. Only a hurricane of truths taking turns bashing into me like bullies reminding me why it was never safe to trust Sonia with what I had left of my fragile heart.

She kissed Talia the night after kissing me. After holding me, crying to me, telling me I was all she wanted. Her emotional blindsides gave me whiplash, and I couldn't see straight, couldn't think. My body shook.

I knew it.

I fucking knew it. God, I'm so stupid.

I imagined the love of my life loving someone else. Intimate moments shared in the dark, her lips on Tallia's hips, declaring them her home. Pain ruptured from my core and shot through my heart. My chin heaved high and my mouth flew open in time for a guttural bellow to rip from my insides. My body shook uncontrollably. My muscles convulsed.

The caddy dropped to the floor, spilling toiletry bottles across the area rug.

I can't...

I heaved a ragged inhale and fell to the rug, gasping for more air before the next image of Sonia in the cozy cave of her room, whispering promises of loyal adoration to Tallia while tangled in her arms, hit my heart from the side like an old piece of metal and dragged itself through me.

A silent cry shoved my chest forward with its force. My palms hit the rug. My fingers dug in. Muscles all though my body squeezed, pulling together against my will, wringing out strength with each knot tying me tighter.

Chills shuddered through me, creeping icicles across my frazzled nerves. An actual cry finally found its way out from under the rubble, releasing tears, the onslaught of rain from the tornado spinning inside.

With weak arms I reached for fallen bottles, my frozen fingers barely registering the plastic's texture. After placing them back into the caddy, I crawled to the bed and hoisted my weight onto shaky legs.

On an intentional inhale, I willed my short breaths to lengthen and walked to the dresser. My fingers tingled from the lack of blood flow with threats of going numb.

Okay, I told myself, not daring to look in the mirror. *Breathe.*

A cry burst from my throat, nearly pushing me back to the floor. I clutched the wooden furniture to keep steady.

Breathe.

Inhale. Exhale. Inhale. Exhale.

I walked to the door and placed my hand on the knob, assessing my ability to make it to the shower room before another sob cracked my chest. The tears weren't going to stop, but the short breaths were lessening. They weren't gone. I could feel them at the edges of my being, waiting.

Inhale. Exhale.

I turned the knob, quickly scanned the empty hallway, and ran for it, caddy in hand. Thankfully, the shower room wasn't too much farther down the hall than my bedroom, and the lights were off when I entered the fully tiled space.

In a panic, I ran to the farthest shower stall, turned the faucet on to hot, and kept out of the water's spray. White and silver tiles, cold and hard, worsened my shaky nerves as I leaned against the stall wall and clawed at the straps on my heels.

The shaking intensified, bringing with it a tight chest and short breaths.

Oh God.

I tossed my shoes outside the stall and tugged my dress up over my head, flinging it, along with my underwear, nearby. Steam rolled toward me when I closed the shower curtain and turned to face the spray of water.

An audible cry crawled from the depths of the well holding my love. In defeat, I pressed my palms into the tile beneath the shower-head and allowed hot liquid to beat down on the crown of my head. Like lava, it seeped into my skin, my bones, soothing the knots in my muscles and my mind.

My worst fears became reality. Picturing Sonia with another unknown woman after we broke up had been hard enough. It was what kept me avoiding her. But having a face and a body and a voice and a whole person...

Well, that brought my fearful imagination into actual existence, as though the images in my head morphed from caricatures to live action. Now I could see the lust in Sonia's eyes, hear her satiated sighs, feel her smile on a kiss of satisfaction with Tallia.

I allowed another cry to fall from my mouth, the ability to control my limbs and lungs returning to me. My shoulders dropped, scooping my back. Streams beat the top of my spine. I intentionally dragged steamy air into my lungs, held on to it, and released it.

Warm arms eased around my back from behind, soft. Her tattooed arms wrapped their way across my chest, pressing in gently, the way she used to help me put myself back into my body during panic attacks.

"May I?" she said.

"Yes," I replied.

In my ear, she slowly breathed in and out, on a cadence meant to guide my own breathing. I matched mine to hers, the rhythm bringing my shoulders to stand upright.

Her naked body pressed into mine, a wall of protection at my back. As though my cells had ached to feel her like this for a year, everything in me melted with relief. I didn't care that I wouldn't get to have her. I had her now, and all I wanted was her.

If I was going to lose her, at least this time I would get to say good-bye. I would get to know it was coming and prepare myself, experience Sonia at every level. I would greedily collect, like photos, the sensation of her fingertips pressed into me, and the security of her arms folded over mine. I would create a mental scrapbook of how good it felt to be loved by Sonia.

But right now, she was here, in my arms, melting under my kisses and touches. And if all I cared about was now, enough to accept any fate with her as long as I could feel her in the present, then why not try for more than memories or what could have been?

If I was going to lose Sonia, this time I would go out swinging.

She released her hold of me and stepped back when I turned. I reached my arms up around her neck and pulled her into the water with me as I pressed my mouth onto hers and reminded her what *my* love felt like.

Our kisses darkened into the kind of passion found in pain, two souls bound to one another beneath the soil and yet kept from blooming topside close enough to touch.

I knotted my fingers at the base of her skull and pressed her lips deeper into mine. In an instant, she grabbed my thighs, hoisting me to her belly. I wrapped my legs around her hips as she backed me into the tile. Her brown eyes, starved for me, flashed with a raw hunger only an animalistic hunt for pleasure could quench.

She buried her face in my breasts as she freed her right hand, leaning my weight onto the wall and her left arm. I allowed my head to lean back, offering of myself whatever her hunt. Her tongue circled my nipple. She sucked hard, nursing a moan from my lips.

With an amplified need, Sonia's mouth moved south, her teeth pressing, her tongue pulling. She gripped my breast with her free hand, squeezing flesh while rubbing her thumb over my nipple.

She eased our bodies lower until my toes touched the floor, and she repositioned herself on her knees in front of me. I wove my fingers up through faded sides to the wave of hair at the top, allowing my nails to drag along her scalp, and gazed at the tops of her sexy broad shoulders.

Another memory to collect and hide away, just in case I wasn't the one she chose after all this. The view of her shoulders, the way her forearms reached across my belly like a seat belt.

Tears filled my eyes. I allowed them to pass as I rested my gaze on the woman I would never get over. I knew it in my bones. If Sonia and I didn't end up together, there was no doubt her ghost would forever haunt the halls of my heart.

So, I collected my possible last memories of Sonia, hoping they'd be enough to feed the inevitable famished aches. Swatches of her to bring me comfort, like a beloved blanket, on days when love stung with the betrayal of knowing it enough to be broken by its power, but not healed by its balm.

My love looked up to lock her gaze onto mine. Her kisses had found their way to my inner thighs, and now her mouth hovered between my legs, her warm breath inviting my pelvis to close the distance.

I mouthed, "I love you."

Her lips smiled against me before her tongue pressed firm and flat, dragging up. She released my breast and made the *I love you* sign with her hand, pressing it into my sternum as I melted into her.

If closure was what I ultimately came to Madrid for, then so be it.

❖

"I never thought I'd get to see this again," Sonia whispered into my hair moments after I opened my eyes.

Sunlight streamed through the part in the floral curtain panels covering Sonia's balcony door and cut a white line across the thin comforter. Concentrated heat brought warmth to my calf, slung over Sonia's legs under the bedding. The only things missing were our dogs, snoring at our feet and backs, between the two of them.

"I only fantasized about it," I said, enjoying the view of our bodies, indiscernible from one another under the blanket, cream fabric lumps.

For a year, Sonia lived in my fantasies, wove herself in and out as the one who showed up one day to make sense of my feelings for her. To confirm for me that yes, she was my person, my soulmate, the reason I couldn't seem to move on.

"What were the fantasies?" Sonia asked, kissing my temple.

I squeezed my arm around her and kissed where my head lay, at the soft spot between her shoulder and her breast. "That we would learn what we needed to learn to be together, and find one another again, make all the pain worth something." I corrected myself. "Worth more than the lessons of it all."

"Hmm," she said, the perfect hint of rasp in her voice. "Sounds like it came true." She drew slow circles along the side of my hip, under the covers.

I watched the cream lump her hand created, thankful to feel her adoring touch.

"I probably don't have the right to say this, but I fantasized about that too," she said.

"Why don't you feel you have a right?" I asked.

"Because I ended us." The painful truth hung like stale smoke. Her hand stilled. She flattened her palm to my thigh. "I knew you were my forever, and I still left you. I wanted you to see past my excuses for breaking up with you, and into the real reasons, when I couldn't even see them at the time."

"What were the real reasons?" I said, afraid to know the answer.

Last night, after the shower, in the throes of making love in her room, apologies were uttered on tears, through kisses, but never explanations. I knew a discussion would take place with the light of day and I hoped not a minute sooner. Spending a last night in her bed, tucking memories away, was how I wanted to spend the night with Sonia.

I had told myself I would allow the discussion to unfold naturally, and I promised I wouldn't avoid when it came. Here I lay, soaking up the way Sonia's skin glided across mine each time her chest rose and fell with breath, upholding my promise.

I tried not to physically stiffen as I inwardly braced myself for her explanation behind ending us.

She exhaled. "I…" She cleared her throat. "I didn't know who I was, suddenly. When my dad died, it was like my foundation split open and the dark chasm enveloped me," she said, her voice cracking at the last part.

I rubbed my hand along her back as far as I could reach, slowly, back and forth, urging her to go on, to open up. These were the truths I wanted from Sonia. Not why she blamed me for her emotions, but the deeper aspects—where in her heart did the pain originate? I could help her with that, show her how thoroughly I supported her. If she would have let me be her cheerleader, I would have, every step of the way, even a slow slog through the mire of grief. I would have.

"Everything," she said on a sniffle. Her chest quivered. "I questioned everything—my spiritual beliefs, my sexuality, my personality. All of it suddenly came up for debate. Who was I without his influence?"

Sonia's voice broke open and sobs spilled out.

I scooted up and leaned on my elbow, pulling her head to the concave between my breasts. She wrapped her arms around my ribs and pressed her face into my chest, as grief bubbled and poured from its confines.

Her ragged inhales led to purging exhales, prompting me to pull her closer, protectively holding space for her to safely remove shards of pain and let me carry their cutting weight awhile.

"He was my world before you. We did everything together. His opinion was the one that mattered. Then I met you. And man, he loved you for me." She said the last bit on a smile she couldn't carry.

"I'm so sorry," I said, crying silently as Sonia courageously exhumed raw emotion. Guilt clawed my gut. She was right. I should have known. I should have assumed the best of her, like I had wanted her to do of me. I should have taken myself out of the equation altogether and automatically held space for her.

"No," she said sharply. "Don't blame yourself. I'm sorry I did that. I shouldn't have. You didn't cause me to freak out when

I realized how much I needed you, how much closer we were growing."

Sonia pushed herself up onto her elbow to look me eye to eye. With her free hand, she stroked a stray hair from my eyelash. "I had to go through it," she said. Tears glistened in the honey folds in her brown eyes.

"Yeah, but you should have gone through it with me," I said, pressing my palm into the widest part of her back until she scooted close enough for our noses to touch. "You're right. I should have known better. I should have been there for you."

"No, you shouldn't have. That was unfair of me to say. If you came into my emergency department bleeding out, I would lose my shit. You think I'd be my normal self, taking charge like it was just another Monday? I'd forget what gauze was, or something."

I smiled at her comparison. I inhaled her validation. Tears filled my eyes on the exhale.

"What's going on, babe?" she asked, grazing her knuckle across each of my cheeks to catch tears.

"It feels like a weight lifted," I said, "to be seen by you. Still wish I would have done things differently, but thank you."

Sonia's gaze seemed to search into me, her brows knit and unknit as she dug and came up to the surface. "Baby, your love terrified me. Daily, I see death at work. In all its unbiased forms and variations. Until it hit me personally, I could keep it at arm's length. It was a work thing, and separating the two wasn't a problem. But then the two tangled. I saw you in the old people with dementia, crying for their dead spouses. You could have been the young woman who came in with a stomach virus and left on hospice. The therapist attacked by her client when she checked in on him."

I remembered the night after she learned her stomach virus patient passed, a week into hospice. She left work, picked up Harriet and a few things, and showed up on my doorstep to sleep at my house. "I wish I would have spent more effort trying to understand your pain and less worrying I was losing you."

Sonia scoffed. "Please. Babe, no." She shook her head, booping her nose to mine in the process. "I got more and more agitated with you, short-tempered. The powerlessness of knowing I could lose you at any moment, and what exactly that kind of loss feels like, mixed with the realization that you were already filling the holes he left in my life. Babe, it left a mess only I could clean up. I had to sort out how I felt and then why I felt it. And I had to do it on my own—I was already questioning how much of my life I based on him more than me." She gave a soft, quick peck on my lips. "I needed to go through each part of me in question, examine it, decide whether it served still or not, and kept or discarded it accordingly. And I needed to do it without interference, so I could trust the new portion of foundation I was building for myself to repair the crack. I had to trust it all came from me."

Sonia pulled me onto her until our bodies lay aligned with one another, the top of my head just below her chin. Her heart beat against my ear, and I silently thanked the universe for her life, her existence, and her place on my path.

"I missed you so damn much," she said on an exhale.

"I missed you," I replied.

"I don't want to spend any more time apart from you here," she said. "Can we officially try again?"

I released an exhale. "Whoa."

"Is it too much? Whatever pace, I'm fine with it. But I don't want to not sit with you anymore. I don't want to pretend you're not the only one here I want to spend any time with. You're the only one I want to go home with."

"It's not too much, but shit." I wiped the back of my index finger across my lower lids, clearing tears before more sprang up to fill their place. "It's everything."

"You're everything, Elly," she said, placing her fingertips beneath my chin. "You have my word I won't run from my everything anymore. I'll only run to you. My dad was right. A love worth sacrificing for isn't just for the fun and companionship. They'll be your balm in life's tough situations. To be with you, to really appreciate what a gift you are, I must also deeply acknowledge the chasm in my life your loss would cause. Acknowledging that is a sacrifice of surface roles, of a fantasy. I must sacrifice my ideal of what love should be, the flimsy version of what it should look like, to carry the heaviness of a deep connection, carved through rupture and repair, to recognize what love is."

She lifted me to place an arm on each side of her, my hands squished into her pillow.

"I love you, Sonia Comstock," I said, finally, after crying it, uttering it, trying to numb it.

"I love you, Elly Straus." She sat up under me and I wrapped my legs around her waist, sitting on her lap. "Does that mean I can be yours in public?"

I laughed at the question. "I would love for you to be mine in public."

"Good."

"Which means we need to talk strategy."

I groaned. "I know."

"I have a violet bundle."

I groaned a second time, more dramatically. "I know."

She laughed. "Damn, you're cute."

"Focus," I joked.

"Impossible when you're in the room," she retorted.

I missed being Sonia's.

"I'm going to talk to Tallia at the cocktail party," she started, all business and sexy smart. "Let her know my feelings and try to convince her that giving my bundle to another contestant would give someone else a chance to know her better."

"And if she says no?" I asked.

"Why would she, though?" she responded. "Why waste my spot on someone she could actually end up with?"

"True."

Chapter Seventeen

Elly

Techno music pulsed and bodies gyrated on the dance floor in Fulanita de Tal, the little lesbian bar Tallia brought us to in Chueca, Madrid's LGBTQ+ district. I stood at the worn wooden bar top, sipping my drink, taking it all in. If Sonia was with me, I decided, the moment would have been perfect.

After the walking tour, over cobblestone streets and through alleys, I deemed my decision to wear a cotton patchwork knee-length skirt and black crop top tank with black Converse a winner. The clip to keep my hair up and off my neck proved helpful too. I styled it that way because Sonia loved it up, and she lay in my bed while I got ready. The stuffy heat made me glad I kept it up.

I lowered my mouth over my straw, enjoying my surroundings of sapphics dancing, talking, laughing, and kissing. If Sonia was here, I thought, we'd be one of those couples making out on the dance floor.

There was a reason this sapphic reality dating show chose Madrid to film their pilot season. Madrid was so queer-friendly that their annual Pride celebration lasted a week, not a weekend like the more progressive cities in the US.

From the looks of the Pride flags hanging through the city and tonight's hopping scene in Chueca, I could tell Madrid was in the midst of preparing for their Pride kickoff party in a couple weeks. And I couldn't wait, after feeling the vibe tonight.

The show's filming itinerary included an all-cast day at Madrid Pride before flying home and waiting the three months to fly to California for the Tell All. I made a mental note to bring Sonia back to this club as the sudden urge to find a dark corner with her filled my thoughts.

Distant memories of a post-sex discussion with Sonia floated through my mind. While still panting from her orgasm, I had crawled higher, onto her stomach, and rested my temple below her breast. She squirmed with sensitive delight under my light touch as I drew hearts on her skin with my fingertip.

"What brought that on?" she had asked, still in the process of catching her breath.

Snow fell lazily out her bedroom window, blanketing the darkness in still silence. Her winter comforter lay rumpled, shoved half off the foot of the mattress. I remembered it being a Saturday night because I was off work that day and she wasn't. She had taken Harriet for scheduled shots Friday, so I stayed at her place Saturday, snuggling the fatigued four-legged baby while her immune system did its thing.

While loving on our little patient curled in my lap on the couch, I read a steamy sapphic romance. Pouncing on Sonia the moment she walked in from work was a mistake I made once, early on in our relationship. She had a routine of stripping her work clothes as soon as she locked the front door behind her. By the time she arrived to her bathroom, she had tossed the wad of dirty laundry as she passed the hamper, and she immediately climbed into the shower for hot water to wash the day off.

That particular Saturday night, I waited as long as it took Sonia to walk from her bathroom to her bedroom, wearing only a towel. She rifled through her dresser for pajamas. I had pounced before she found what she was looking for and after her towel fell to the floor.

"What brought on my need to feel my love's warmth against mine?" I asked innocently. My heart-drawing on her belly paused as I considered how many details to give her. "I read this book today…"

Sonia's stomach muscles tightened beneath my cheek as she chuckled. "Why am I not shocked?"

We lay, connected, in the quiet darkness of her bedroom. Traces of light from the bathroom's open door down the hall barely illuminated the progressive rainbow flag and framed pictures of us on her wall. She absently ran her fingers through my hair.

"What was this one about?" she asked. "Or do I not want to know? Will it give away tonight's ending?"

"Ha!" I said from my comfy spot near her ribs. From that vantage point, I could breathe in her fresh clean scent, feel the warmth of her skin, gaze at her round curves and straight edges. "Kitty's is already closed." Sonia's shift ended after last call.

Her orgasmic cloud of pleasure must have begun clearing, because her hand stilled on my scalp. "Babe, are you talking about sex in public, because…"

I laughed and kissed her belly. "It was hot, baby." I considered why the idea of doing private things with her in public was suddenly an invigorating idea. Being seen by others had been more of a deterrent than a turn-on, so my fantasy had nothing to do with that.

After a short six-month stint gorging all things sapphic smut, I went back to my reading norms of fantasy subgenres and stopped wondering what it was about Sonia that made me sexually adventurous. My sex therapist friend had suggested I was simply experiencing the beautiful unfurling of pleasure that happened when lovers found safety and security in each other. Of course the safety aspect, enabling me to try new things, had been part of it. But there was also more I couldn't wrap my head around.

Years later, I stood in a sapphic nightclub full of hidden corners. The series of rooms, all connected, included alcoves and angles. The front reminded me of an old theater's narrow box-office booth, complete with glass swinging door. From where I stood, I counted four different wall colors including a white wall with black polka dots, and neon signs. One read *The future is female* in bright pink.

My sapphic smut stint flickered to life in my memories, painted with new details granted by time and distance. My sex therapist friend had been more correct than I'd given her credit for, only with a distinct twist that kept me from grasping her opinion as helpful insight.

Yes, Sonia and I had been growing deeper in our intimacy that winter, which gave me the confidence to try new things, including pleasure. But it had been more than lust and confidence fueling those desires. I understood now.

Back then, I wanted more from her without realizing it. I sensed us growing together, deepening our combined roots, and it thrilled me, the possibilities of us, how far we could soar lifting one another. So, I pressed for more, to keep pushing past prior limits, hand in hand.

Sonia met me with resistance. Which understandably turned to a solid wall when her dad got sick the first time. The treatment worked, he screened cancer-free, we all went back to life as usual, but Sonia couldn't. She carried the fear of his cancer returning like a boulder across her shoulders, unable to put it down, and eventually unable to notice she carried it.

When his cancer returned with a vengeance, the mental load Sonia lugged around, day in and day out, overtook her. And the boulder between us solidified.

My observations were void of blame. Sometimes life happened, and the best a person could do was navigate the changing landscape through enough introspection to redesign their own inner landscape.

If Sonia and I lasted through filming, to the all-cast Madrid Pride, I vowed to put the moves on her here. Not out of lust or a deepening sense of self-confidence urging me to try new things, but because I wanted to build memories with her. The kind that created steel beams from shared laughter and metal meshing from new, exciting experiences. A foundation of love and trust so strong that not even death could shake it apart.

"Drinking to forget?" Beth asked, sliding up beside me at the bar. They offered their raised glass and I lifted mine in a cheers. They wore their signature short slacks—tonight's pair were light pastel green—with a short-sleeve black V-neck.

"It was an intense night," I agreed, shifting my thoughts to the group date. Kamal hadn't been wrong in his description of the walking tour. We learned bits of Madrid's dark history. "What messed with you the worst?"

Beth looked up for a few breaths before seeming to settle on an answer. "The Inquisition stuff. It was like the more they showed, the deeper it got, the darker, the more it reminded me of the recent tactics used to oppress marginalized groups."

I nodded. "Me too." I took a sip at the thought. "When will people realize othering groups of humans *always* ends up on the wrong side of history?"

I didn't give Beth a chance to say anything before I added another thought. The tour got my head working, and I couldn't stop the flow of opinions now. I appreciated the conversation.

"Look at us all, for example," I said. "I'm sure there's more than a couple different countries represented in this bar tonight. And lots of nationalities and ethnicities. Some are from around here, some are tourists or here for another reason. All likely have a connection to being queer. Our LGBTQ-plus family is worldwide, and probably one of the most loving, accepting, and big-hearted families in existence. For the most part, we try to build bridges, not walls. And I think that's the whole point. Tonight was a rough reminder of what happens when we focus on building walls. People become sorted into roles they must conform to, and no one wins."

Beth clapped. "If we were buying our own drinks tonight, I'd buy you one, Elly. That was soapbox worthy. Preach." They raised their glass.

I smiled and took another drink. Sapphic nightclubs were always my happy places. Warm tingles joined the pulsing music, like they were their own little individual notes dancing in my bloodstream, feeding my muscles. I continued sipping while my lower half shimmied along with the song, until my straw drew up air and bits of melting ice.

My feet shifted and my hips swayed with the new beat as techno music melded into an upbeat pop song I always *had* to dance to. "I gotta dance! I'll be back."

Beth raised their glass and gave a nod.

I wove through the crowd to find a space on the dance floor.

Lights of all colors took turns illuminating through the dark room, picking apart our smooth movements as more dancers undulated with each flash. Sweat and perfume filled the air.

I let the music take me. With my eyes closed to feel the beat pulsing through my veins, I replayed the evening's events, curious whose bed Sonia and I would be lying in together when I summarized tonight's group date for her.

Each of us had spent alone time with Tallia on this date. During my time with her, she asked questions that gave me the impression she was more interested in who my ex was than in me. Considering she chose Sonia for her first one-on-one, and on that date they shared a kiss, I had a pretty good idea about the information she sought.

As though Tallia knew I was thinking about her, she moved into my line of sight, seemingly lost in the moment with Heather as they danced, slow and seductive, to a fast-paced song.

Tallia literally had her pick of partners at the villa. As far as I knew, Sonia and I were the only exes here still romantically involved. LeeAnn and Michelle didn't announce their past connection to the group, but over the course of today's tour it had become known.

It started as a little inconsequential argument over tapas that could have happened between any two contestants following back-to-back nights of partying in a romantic pressure-cooker. Michelle made a snarky comment about LeeAnn taking the last of her favorite dish, on purpose. When LeeAnn replied with a smartass quip about always being clear about who she was and what she wanted, which Michelle had known about her from the beginning, the group knew the two weren't discussing tapas.

Maybe I was being judgy, but I didn't see LeeAnn and Michelle trying to work anything out. I saw them equal parts irritated and thankful the other happened to be there to get in the way and also help them feel not so alone.

Yet our bacheloress didn't seem to have any qualms with their openly messy skeletons. While in line for the bathroom, LeeAnn and Michelle stood a few people in front of me, making out.

Not long after that, while I sipped drinks and chatted with Beth at the bar, I saw the two of them outside the open front door to the club, on the street, arguing with hands flailing. A few minutes earlier, sometime after their PDA in the bathroom line, LeeAnn had been making out with Tallia on the dance floor. And now Tallia nearly did the same with Heather.

So why, when Tallia and I had our alone time to talk, after trying unsuccessfully to shift her focus multiple times, did she only want to ask about why things between my ex and me didn't work out?

Chapter Eighteen

Sonia

Sunblock and towel in hand, I made my way to a single lounge chair in the sun. I lowered the bill of my ball cap and closed my eyes. The sun's warmth seeped into my skin. Two nights in a row of hardly any sleep, tossing and turning, had a way of creating knots.

Back when Elly and I were together, she either texted after a night out or she came to my house and crawled into my bed. Either of those would have been perfect last night. I wished I could have gotten a text with a selfie of her in her pj's and rainbow glasses, doing whatever random nightly task she happened to be in the middle of while messaging me.

I had tried to stay awake but fell asleep while waiting for the carpool van's headlights to come up the villa's driveway and into my room from the balcony. The late nights and heavy emotions were getting to me, wearing me down.

Even then, when I woke and the digital clock in my room said it was nearly three in the morning, I wished we could have our phones. If I had my phone, I would have checked to see Elly's *good night* text to know she was sleeping safely in her bed and I could relax.

It all came down to her, didn't it? It always had.

Something deep inside told me it always would too.

I groaned inwardly, thinking about my one-on-one with Tallia. The kiss felt wrong.

But Elly. Elly felt right. It took getting on a plane and flying all the way to Spain to find that out. Just like it took a drive to Seattle for a sapphic prom to meet her.

From the moment I saw her here, I wished she and I had the villa to ourselves. On an anniversary or our honeymoon. Not clocking one another from afar, acting like we didn't get to choose our own futures.

If anything, that was what I woke up thinking this morning. That I had the freedom to choose for myself. I chose three a.m. *good night* texts, and walks through Manito Park, and hot wordless showers where the water was scalding too.

I chose Elly and hoped, after her group date, she still chose me.

"Elly! Finally!" someone yelled from the pool.

I lifted the brim of my hat. LeeAnn stood waist-high in the pool. Sapphire sat on the pool's edge beside her, legs dangling in the cool water.

Elly's shins entered my line of sight, and I relished the way her muscles shifted and flexed as her wooden sandals clomped across the cement toward me. In the shower, I had traced her new floral tattoo, winding up her calf to her lower thigh, with my lips. I smiled at the memory.

"Wanna chat over coffee?" Elly asked with a smile in her voice that made me smile.

LeeAnn splashed toward us and Elly yelled, "Yeah, no, didn't ask to get wet before my first coffee of the day, thanks."

"Hey, any time's a good time to get wet," LeeAnn quipped back.

I already didn't like LeeAnn. That comment made me want to swim circles around her dumb ass with knowledge. No one wanted to be talked to like that. Her disrespect for others grated on me. When she pointed it at Elly...*grated* wasn't the word, and swimming with knowledge wasn't entirely what I imagined.

"That's gross," Elly said.

"Yeah," I said, standing to gather my things. "Let's go inside." I shook my head at LeeAnn as we passed the pool.

"So how did it go last night?" I asked once we found comfortable spots on a couch in the living room, having detoured to the kitchen for our coffees.

Elly sat at the far end of the beige couch, her legs folded and lower back touching the armrest as she faced me beside her. God, she looked amazing in the morning.

Beth and Katy joked and danced while they cleaned the morning's breakfast mess in the kitchen. They paid us no attention. Pop music played from a speaker mounted onto the side of a cabinet as Beth washed dishes and Katy cleared dirty dishes and condiments from the island and dining room table.

The background noise of music, laughing, and dishes clanking helped to cloak our conversation.

"Weird," Elly said after finishing a sip. She winced and blew the hot liquid. "None of us got a lot of alone time with Tallia, but I doubt anyone's was like mine."

"How so?" I asked, curious how similar or different her experience with Tallia had been to mine.

"Babe, I resorted to asking her favorite movie." Elly paused for effect. "Her. Favorite. Movie. You know I don't give a shit about movies, but she kept asking about my last relationship and why did it end and maybe I wasn't ready for a new one, and how did I feel with my ex being here. Basically, she asked everything but who my ex was."

I groaned. This was what I was afraid of after our one-on-one, when I had time to replay it all, detail by detail. I had hoped my lack of a kiss, when Tallia went in for a second, expressed where I stood when it came to her and me. When she ended the date early, I figured she picked up what I was putting down.

But I also knew my hopes weren't the only options for how Tallia would respond.

"Were you able to get a read on where her head's at?" I asked.

The bun Elly arranged nightly in place with a scrunchie now hung loose while blond wisps stuck out with no rhyme or reason. Elly shook her head, flopping the bun looser.

"No, and LeeAnn and Michelle kind of came out as exes last night. Tallia didn't seem to give two shits about that."

"What's her deal?"

"Literally." Elly's rainbow frames slid down her nose when she attempted another sip of coffee. She pushed them back up, and I thanked the universe I got to see them on her again, in person. "Pretty sure Tallia made out with most of the contestants last night too. If she has a favorite, I have no clue who it is."

I hoped it wasn't me. It would make no sense.

"What if you're her favorite?" Elly asked, leaning in, as though she read my mind. Sometimes I thought she did, with how connected we were.

"I need to make sure that I'm not," I answered.

"I missed you so much last night," Elly continued, leaning forward. She placed a hand on my thigh. "I can't leave tonight. Not without you. I just got you back."

My heart fluttered from Elly's confirming words.

"I'll fix this," I said, wishing, for the thousandth time, that I hadn't let Tallia kiss me. "I'm planning to talk to her tonight, before the violet ceremony. Let her know where I stand and that she's better off filling my spot with someone she has a chance with. I've been going over different scenarios and how I'll handle them."

Elly gave a half smile and a nod.

"Hey," I said, grabbing her hand to hold in mine. "I'm not letting you go again. No matter what happens here tonight, at the end of this all we're both going back to Spokane. We're both committed to making this work. No matter what happens tonight, I am yours. Know that."

A smile tugged the corner of her mouth up slowly, as though she was afraid to trust it. She stood, and I mirrored her, placing my coffee on the little side table, next to hers. She yawned and stretched her arms up and out. I took the opportunity to wrap my arms around her waist and pick her up.

Elly squealed and laughed as I spun us in a circle, nuzzling my cheek to her chest. I brought her down enough for her feet to touch the floor and planted kisses all over her cheeks before releasing her.

"Good," she said, pretending to shake her head at me as she slid her feet into her wooden sandals. "Does this mean we don't have to argue first to recreate the other night, if I want to get you in the shower with me?"

I sucked in my breath, not at all prepared for that to come out of Elly's mouth.

"Well"—I cleared my throat—"we both have to get ready for the violet ceremony's preparty, and that means showers for both of us. I don't see the point in wasting water."

She laughed and slapped my butt as we made our way to the entry and toward the stairway. "Our showers do the opposite of saving water."

The response popped into my mind, but I didn't say the embarrassing statement aloud.

You save me, Elly Straus.

Chapter Nineteen

Elly

The confession room looked different through the clarity of sobriety. The small space that was probably once a large storage closet felt cozy and inviting between eggplant purple walls, the salt lamp, and the sporadic placement of violet and rainbow art and potted plants.

It took me a minute to think of anything to share as I sat uncomfortably on the same love seat I kissed Sonia on. And to increase my discomfort, my butt slid into the crack where the two red couch cushions met, thanks to my dress's satin fabric.

Repositioning myself meant I had to go through the process of fixing myself again, patting down the wrinkles in my dress, the flyways in my hair.

After hours with Sonia, as we got ready for the violet ceremony, the moment had arrived. The sea of thoughts swimming in my head were all about her. She wasn't a school of fish. She was the whole ocean.

Chatting with her over coffee on the couch this morning, in full view of anyone who happened by, nourished my soul in a way I hadn't realized. It really was the simple things, wasn't it? Like finding secret moments in public to create a magic only the two of us could see.

When most people imagined a future romantic relationship, it was the little things they tended to want. The companionship, someone to come home to, to share dinners with, to be lazy or adventurous with. And yet, once we got comfortable in a relationship, those aspects diminished in importance, replaced by the occurrences involving bigger emotions, scarier stakes.

"I think," I said, trying to start again at stating a complete thought that made sense. "I think I need to give more credit to the smaller moments in the future."

When I had been in this room with Sonia, the little circular camera perched on a black narrow stand across from the love seat was inconsequential. I didn't remember noticing it. With the lights on, I saw why. It reminded me of a desktop computer's aftermarket addition, clipped to the top of a flat screen or something, void of any distinguishable quality including a recording light.

It occurred to me that it could have recorded Sonia and me.

It also occurred to me that I didn't care if the world saw our love, as long as I willed myself to forget the me-being-embarrassingly-tipsy part.

Why did Sonia always have to feel like home? This trip was the farthest distance I'd traveled, and yet here Sonia was to give me home. How could she be both everything I needed and also the person who left me like I meant nothing?

"But I guess that's not a big deal," I muttered to the little camera tasked at collecting my secrets. Walking into this room, I made it my goal to keep the camera starved while also giving it enough time to appease Elise's insistence that I try to get more confession time in.

I came on this show to represent queer joy and to see if I could maybe fall in love. Not to bare my soul to strangers.

I started talking again about my thoughts on tonight's violet ceremony. How Shay was either going to come back from her one-on-one brunch with a violet bundle, or she wasn't going to come back at all.

I left out my thoughts on Sonia's bundle of violets.

I shared that I didn't expect to sleep at the villa tonight because Tallia seemed cold toward me during on group date. Her questions during our brief alone time on the date weren't curious. She was trying to fill in the holes to a story she already assumed about me. It felt different from our interactions during the first couple nights.

When I ran out of facts for the little unassuming camera, I wrapped it up and left the confession room.

I felt lighter inside, the way someone anticipated visiting the place they knew their crush would be. Coming to Madrid to crush on Sonia felt like a great reason for the trip.

Phantom memories of her hands on me, where they belonged, made me flush with tingles racing under my skin. It was all real, too. I got to feel Sonia's arms wrapped around me. Got to breathe her in. I couldn't wait to be wrapped up in her again tonight, after the ceremony, at the wellness retreat together.

"You look happy," Sapphire said, looking me up and down the moment her heeled foot hit the tiled entry from the stairs. "Different."

"Thanks?" I said playfully.

She looped her arm in mine as we walked toward the living room. "I take it you're feeling confident about tonight."

I took a drink of my water bottle and shot a quick glance around the kitchen for Sonia. I was eager to be by her side again.

"The violet ceremony? I'm not the least bit confident." I peeked out the glass double doors leading to the pool patio from the living room and saw no one. Rolling carts of snacks and cocktail ingredients sat on the patio, each decorated with twinkly lights in the late evening twilight.

"You think you're going home tonight?" Sapphire asked.

"Going to the wellness retreat?" I said jokingly. "Probably."

It occurred to me that while I felt relaxed, Sapphire did not. She wrung her hands at her waist, probably without even realizing. "Why?" she asked.

Nervous energy pinged through me as I focused on Sapphire and kept my senses alert for Sonia.

"Tallia felt off to me at our group date," I answered absently, then realized we never caught up after our group dates. "How was *your* group date, by the way?"

Sapphire rolled her eyes. "Renee was so irritating. I honestly hope Tallia sends her away because I don't know if I can live through another group anything with that individual."

"What did she do?" I asked.

Heather walked into the kitchen from the dining room, got a glass from a cupboard, and filled it with water from the fridge.

"Hey," I said, standing at the white granite countertop separating the living room from the kitchen. "Where's everyone? Are they still getting ready for tonight?"

Heather looked at the clock on the microwave. Her bright red hair reminded me of fire cascading down one side of her face, spilling onto her shoulder, while the other side sported a shaved style. She pointed to the hall she came from. "Figured karaoke was a good way to let off some steam before tonight's elimination." She waved the glass of water. "Thirsty, just finished singing a song someone else had on their list that I had no right singing." She left for the game room.

We followed, entering the darkened game room shortly after Heather.

"We've got two more!" someone called.

We made our way to the couch at the far end of the huge room and parted to sit in the few empty spots left. Sonia looked up and shot me a comforting smile. After a painful year of being apart from her, I got to have her in my life again. Hopefully for the rest of my life.

"Hi," I mouthed to her. I should have known to check the game room for her.

Sonia and Beth scooted enough to create an empty spot between them for me.

I sat and placed my water bottle on the floor between my feet. The room smelled like tanning oil, sunscreen, cologne, perfume, and alcohol, but with the airy clean scent of a large, well-kept home.

"Any song requests?" Katy asked of the room's newest members, manning the karaoke station like she had the other night. The night Sonia walked in on me singing our apocalyptic get-back-together song.

Katy sat on an ottoman near the left of the mounted TV and box speakers beneath, remotes and an instructional notebook on the remaining cushion space in front of her.

"I'm ready," Sonia responded. "That one."

Katy gave a nod and went back to using one of the remotes to flip through song files on the TV.

"All right, Sonia," Katy announced, not turning to look at us. "You're up."

Sonia slowly stood and straightened her dress slacks. She cleared her throat, grabbed the microphone from Katy, and let the thing hang from her hand as she addressed the group.

"So, when I put this song on my list, what seems like forever long ago," she started.

A couple people chuckled.

Sonia gave a nod. "Yeah, so when I added this as one of my karaoke songs, I also prepared to explain why. I chose this song because I know it, word-for-word, without lyrics on a screen. The day I heard this song, I couldn't stop singing it. A lot of life has happened since then, and I'm still singing it. So."

She nodded at Katy who pressed the remote she held pointed at the TV.

A familiar tune began, and I knew. It wasn't a song we shared, or one I saw on her social media story during a pathetic stalking session. But this was our song.

Because I could sing along without lyrics too.

My heartbeat quickened as the tune began.

Sonia's perfectly gravelly voice began solid, low, dark, and grew in emotional melody as words left her lips, as she sang a Dermot Kennedy song about capturing memories of love to cling to when time parted the lovers.

How often had I bawled to this song, wishing I could dance to it with her, secure in her arms, no longer victims of heartbreak, clamoring for shreds of what we once had, what we once were.

She turned away from the TV and toward the couch, with eyes closed and face turned up. She clutched the microphone like I wished she could clutch me. Her brow furrowed with need and pain and longing.

She looked how I felt.

Part of me wanted to close my eyes and feel the song with her, wished I could wrap my arms around her waist and press into her, the vibrations of her voice moving through me. That was what I used to do when she sang karaoke.

But that's not what we agreed on for tonight, not what we lay in bed earlier today discussing. Tonight, Sonia wanted all Tallia's flak. She wanted to be the one making the grand statement of love because she was the only one entering the elimination ceremony with a bundle of violets pinned to the lapel of her suit jacket.

So I watched, transfixed on the woman only feet away from me, swaying with the tune, singing about desire beside a lake.

Our sunny days at the lake danced in my memory, as Sonia danced in my present. Those not-so-relaxing mornings of packing up the cooler and the car led to glorious hours of lying around and chatting, soaking up summer. It was still summer. After we got home, we could have that again.

Sonia opened her eyes to look at me as she belted out a line about having one last kiss, as though she was going to grab me and show them all what that kind of kiss looked like. She neared me enough to drag a knuckle gently along my cheekbone before pulling back with a flirtatious *gotcha* smile.

Fire seared for her from deep in my abdomen. Only Sonia had the ability to stoke my flames this way. Only her touch held the passion to satiate me. Sinking into the couch, I sat up, moving my body in time with hers, reliving snuggling into her under fireworks beside the lake and meaningful, slow dances in the kitchen or on her patio. Each of those were moments when two souls truly plugged in to one another and created new connections.

I couldn't wait to go home and pick up where we left off. First, though, we needed to get through tonight until we were at the wellness retreat together, nodding off in one another's arms.

After she had broken up with me, especially the way it all happened, I thought she didn't like me, who I was at my core. It made no sense, because she had talked so much about all the things she loved about me.

And then, suddenly, she didn't.

Her adoration rotted into reasons I wasn't right for her.

I had questioned those connections I remembered feeling. Had I fantasized those? Had they not been mutual?

Eventually, I came to the conclusion that a connection like that takes two. It hadn't just been a creation of my mind. I also knew that I would tuck the memories of that once-in-a-lifetime love safely in the spot in my heart reserved for her. I would consider myself lucky for getting to know what that felt like.

I never imagined I would get to watch her sing again, smell the way her cologne mixed with her pheromones, feel her touch, hear her voice. Again.

And now I knew. I didn't have to wonder how she felt about me. I didn't have to avoid her around Spokane or even the villa. The hard part, the part where we had to learn on our own, was past us now. Our time apart belonged in the rearview mirror.

Sonia locked eyes with me as she sang the last chorus, lines I used to bitterly sing-scream in my car while tears streaked my cheeks. Lines promising that no matter what happened to us, our love would never end.

Sonia handed the microphone to Katy, allowing the karaoke track to play the melody out. She held out her hand to me, and I stood to take it. Pulling me into an embrace, Sonia made a show of dipping me back and planting her lips on mine, for all the contestants and camerapeople to see.

The entertained spectators stood, clapping and hooting.

My cheeks ached from smiling. Finally. Finally, I had my Sonia back. I relished the moment, her quickly beating heart against me, the way her rapid breath slowed as she tried to catch it. The way it felt like all was right in the world while in her embrace.

Beth patted Sonia on the back. "It's about damn time, you two."

I smiled as our housemates rallied around us, shocked at their supportive responses. Tingles flooded my body, the elation of watching my fantasies become reality.

"Okay, who's up next?" Katy asked the crowd, their excitement quieting down.

When no one offered their talents, Beth said, "No one wants to follow that act."

Beth's comment garnered laughs.

Someone clapped, a little too slow and late, from the game room's opened doors. All eyes found the bacheloress as she neared the couch, still clapping awkwardly. She dropped her arms and froze halfway to the couch.

"Sonia, can I steal you for a little while?" she asked.

Someone gasped dramatically, but no one said anything.

"It's nothing major," she added. "I'd like to talk to you before the ceremony."

Tallia waited until Sonia kissed me, released me from her embrace, and made her way to her. Nearing the doors, Sonia turned back, caught my gaze for half a second, gave a wink, and left with Tallia, my ex following the bacheloress silently.

CHAPTER TWENTY

Elly

I stood in what we called the violet room, as one of eleven contestants separated out to what I assumed was supposed to be three rows of four. The bottom row was missing a person.

I shifted in my spot on the third and highest row, deciding my platform heels were a risky choice. Why they chose to put the short woman in the back instead of the front, I wasn't sure. At least this time I'd opted for a fitted dress instead of a flowy one. Less chance of tripping on it while trying to get down.

Elise had popped into the game room about ten minutes after Tallia and Sonia left to instruct us to make our way toward the elimination room, her dramatic way of describing the violet room. Tallia had decided to skip the rest of the party and barrel right into the kicking-off part. Else hadn't used those words, but that's what I gathered.

I looked to Sapphire, who stood on the second row. She wore a sleek deep, dark pink sleeve of a dress that somehow almost looked black in the dim lighting.

Candles burned on tables, in clusters, in corners, and along walls—from standing on the floor to hanging from the ceiling. The show's decorators created a dark atmospheric space of intimate sapphic love. I wondered how much better my surroundings would look from the other side of the TV screen. Dreamy, I imagined, with wall-mounted sconces of dangling violets clustered at the stems and tiers of well-dressed people vying for love.

"They know we're in here, right?" Renee snarked.

"I'm starting to wonder," LeeAnn added.

I held back a scoff. The two group-date Tallia hogs. Of course they each had something critical to say. Impatience wound itself up and down my spine. I stretched and shifted in place to keep the jitters at bay.

Sonia and I had created a plan that seemed to be working, but I wondered. What could they be talking about for over twenty minutes? Maybe Sonia's attempt at convincing Tallia went horribly sideways. What if Tallia got so mad she sent Sonia home, and not to the wellness retreat?

"Do you think she's kicking Sonia off?" Michelle asked no one in particular.

"Why? You'll miss her?" LeeAnn asked Michelle in a snarky tone.

"Sonia's Michelle's number two," Renee told Michelle's ex, along with the rest of the group.

"Hey," Michelle scolded. "That was said in confidence."

"It was said with a microphone on," Renee pointed out, before directing her attention back at the others. "She has a list. Tallia is one. Sonia is two. I'm three, Beth is four, Katy is five. Should I go on?"

Michelle covered her face with both hands. Heather, who stood beside her on the third row, gave her a half hug.

The double doors swung open with a swoosh, and camerapeople hurried in wearing all black, carrying recording devices, big fluffy mics, and tripods. Our group quieted, watching.

A couple days ago, someone would have chanced asking a cameraperson a show question. And they would have been ignored for the umpteenth time. At some point we stopped asking and just waited. I felt like a second grader waiting for the flash of class pictures.

It didn't take long for spotlighting to illuminate the room.

Kamal swept in, causing the candles to dance. "Hello, hello, hello! How have you all been?" He made a show of inhaling a bundle of violets and lavender draped from a wall sconce. "Mmmmm. Not my preferred flower, but I can still appreciate its scent and beauty."

A few contestants laughed.

I looked toward the door for signs of Sonia.

"How are you doing, Shay?" Kamal asked, shifting his eyebrows up and down suggestively. "I see you have your violet bundle from today's brunch date. I assume it went well?"

I totally forgot Shay was on a one-on-one today. I wondered if that had anything to do with Tallia wanting to talk to Sonia. If Tallia finished her date with Shay with decisions made.

What kind, though?

Shay gave an embarrassed laugh and lifted her fresh bundle. "You could say that."

"How's it feel? To hold that violet bundle?" Kamal asked.

Shay exhaled loudly. "It feels amazing. I'm lucky to be able to get the chance to know Tallia a few more days longer. And we'll see from there."

What a mature answer, I thought and decided, other than Sapphire and Beth, Shay could be good for Tallia too. I added her to my list of preferred winners.

"Well," Kamal said, putting distance between him and the platform we stood upon, "I bet you're wondering where your other lucky violet holder is. Sonia?"

Sonia walked through the door and entered the decorated portion of the room with us. She looked stunning, her dark hair slicked back, her tan skin glowing, tattoos declaring her beliefs, wearing a light blue short-sleeve polo and light brown slacks with brown leather shoes. She clutched her violet bundle, though hers flopped to one side, unlike Shay's. I supposed she decided not to wear the suit jacket with her violet bundle attached to the lapel and wondered why. Then I remembered our plan.

Why does Sonia still have her violet bundle?

Her brown eyes pierced mine before she took the empty spot

directly below me on the first row. Of course she smelled amazing. The waft of her presence reached my tier shortly after she stood in place, and I nearly melted down to her.

I waited for Kamal to ask Sonia how it felt to be safe tonight. But he never did. He didn't ask her anything.

"Well, now that the gang's all here," Kamal announced, "I think we're ready for the wise and beautiful Tallia."

My fellow contestants clapped as Tallia made her way into the room and in front of the platform we stood upon. She took her place beside Kamal.

"My, my, aren't you an eye-catcher," Kamal said, complimenting the bacheloress.

She gave a curtsy. "Thank you."

Kamal wasn't wrong. Tallia's air of sophistication matched the black pants outfit she wore, with a thick vertical line of sparkling stones down the side of each leg. The top she wore covered one shoulder in a triangle of matching black fabric lined with the same stones.

"Well," Kamal said to Tallia. "Let's get this over with, shall we?"

Kamal stepped back and to the side, out of the way.

"Thank you," Tallia said solemnly. She walked to stand beside an antique wooden table with a platter of violet bundles tied in purple ribbons. She rested her hand on the sturdy piece of furniture.

"First," she began, addressing the three tiers of people, "I want to apologize for shortening the party tonight. The last few days have been eye-opening and exhausting." She put her hand up to cup around her mouth like she was telling us a secret. "I know this is the first time they're doing this, but I'm going to heavily suggest next season they don't schedule so many back-to-back dates for the poor bacheloress."

The group chuckled and made sounds of anxious agreement.

I could have sworn Tallia shot a stabbing glare at me. I looked to Sapphire to see if she noticed. Nope.

Tallia sighed. "So, I'm a big believer in some things. Honor. Clarity. Honesty. Kindness. Thoughtfulness." She shook her head as she studied her hand on the table. "With my friends and chosen family, these attributes can come in all variations. But with my partner, our perceptions of these things need to align."

Tallia removed her hand from the table and paced. "That is one part of my reasoning behind tonight's decisions." She paused to regard us all. "Sometimes these values of mine seem to conflict with one another. Like my need for honoring previously agreed upon commitments and also my need to be honest. Thank you for being flexible enough for me to do what I need to do to stick as close to my values as I can during this experience."

She stopped by the violet bundle–covered table. "And so, with that"—she picked up the first violet bundle of the evening—"I would like to begin tonight's ceremony by saying I am truly sorry to those who were cheated out of time with me, and as a result leaving tonight. I would have liked to have gotten to know you better, but others in this house have different values. Ones that don't include honesty and honor. Or at least how I would perceive them."

Tallia cleared her throat. "LeeAnn, will you accept these violets?"

LeeAnn hopped off the platform in her black Vans and fitted plaid ankle-length slacks. Tallia handed her the bundle, and she wrapped her arms around the bacheloress, whispering into her ear. Tallia smiled and thanked her.

When LeeAnn found her place, Tallia continued, "Beth, will you accept these violets?"

"Oh man," Beth said in surprise as they made their way down the platform. "Of course," they said as they took the bundle. "I'd be honored."

Tallia gave them a hug. She called Heather and then Katy. I tried not to be obvious as I continued a rotation with my eyes, looking at Tallia, Sonia, Sapphire, Tallia again. My new friend's shoulders slumped lower with each name called. She had worried Renee hogging their group date could have cost her a violet bundle. I hoped she was wrong, because Sapphire proved to be a genuine person Tallia would be lucky to call her own.

I was too focused on Sonia to keep track of the count of violet bundles to bodies on the platform, until Kamal joined Tallia near the table to remind us that only one bunch of violets remained.

"There were a total of seven violet bundles, spots in the next round," Kamal said. "Two were given during one-on-one dates. Four have been given already tonight. Tallia, you have one more slot open in the next round, where the dates will be more extravagant, the conversations will be deeper, and the alone time more intimate. Who is moving on with you? Who do you want to know better?"

Tallia picked up the bundle.

Wait, I wanted to jump from the platform and scream, *you forgot to take Sonia's bundle! She doesn't want it! Take it back!*

Panic's icy fingers trailed the back of my neck. My teeth started to rattle. I clamped my jaw shut and balled my fists. *I just got Sonia back.*

There were seven of us on the platform with empty hands. And only one more bundle left. If I didn't get it, I would have to say good-bye to Sonia. Again.

I squeezed my eyes shut in anticipation and then opened them again because what if it was the last time I saw Sonia for the rest of filming? I could only see the back of her head and shoulders, but that was better than nothing. At least I still got to be near her. Still knew when she laughed and when she hurt.

"Sapphire," Tallia said in a clear, strong voice. "Will you accept these violets?"

Sapphire gasped and held her hand over her mouth as she carefully stepped down to the floor. "Yes, thank you so much. I was so worried."

Tallia wrapped her arm around Sapphire in a quick hug. "I'm sorry I made you wait for last."

"It's okay," Sapphire assured her, walking back to us. "As long as you called my name, I don't care if it's last."

Kamal rejoined Tallia when everyone settled. "I'm sorry to those not chosen. Please say your good-byes and leave the villa. Your luggage has already been removed from the grounds."

Like I'd just been blinded by oncoming headlights, I nearly

tripped trying to get off the top tier of the platform. Sonia turned around from the bottom row and held out her arm.

Our eyes caught. I clutched her forearm with one hand and used my other to steady my descent. Heat burned between us.

"I'm sorry," she whispered. "I tried."

When my platforms hit the tile floor, Sapphire wrapped her arms around me, and I let go of Sonia.

"I'm so sorry to see you go," she said, crying on my shoulder. "You're my favorite person here."

I hugged Sapphire back, while watching over her shoulder as Sonia hugged Toren.

Pulling out of her embrace, I fought my raging emotions to focus on Sapphire's happiness. "You deserve to be here," I said, gripping her biceps. "You're a catch, and clearly Tallia knows that." I hugged her again. "So beat their asses, okay?"

"Thank you," she said, wiping a tear from her eye. "I'll see you at the massive Pride party, if I don't get kicked off before then."

Toren passed, and Sapphire reached out to snag them in a good-bye hug.

I searched the crowded space for Sonia.

Beth reached an arm around my shoulder to pull me into a hug. "It's okay if I hug you, right?" they asked. Beth leaned in to speak barely audibly into my ear, probably too quiet for the microphone necklaces we wore to pick up. "Don't let what you and Sonia have slide through your fingers."

They turned away to get a hug from Heidi.

Michelle cried to Sonia.

What was I supposed to do? Walk out? Get into the car and leave?

Just leave Sonia?

My legs refused to budge, refused to act like walking away from her didn't tear my heart out.

My fellow violetless contestants began leaving the room through the double doors for the last time. I looked for Sonia. I had to go, but I couldn't walk away from her without saying good-bye. Without feeling her again.

But I couldn't spot her. And only Renee lingered near Tallia. I expected producers to tell her to leave any minute.

Sonia's arms wrapped around me from behind, and I turned into her embrace. I exhaled into her neck. My home. I inhaled her. Sonia was my oxygen. Something about the air around her, breathing it made me happier.

Able to release my fear and worry in the safety of her embrace, tears sprang to my eyes. "I can't," was all I could mutter around the lump in my throat. "I just got you back."

She squeezed tighter, leaning her cheek on the top of my head. Tears fell onto my forehead. "I tried, baby. It only made her dig in more."

"What's her problem?" I asked, not caring who heard nearby. "She knows she doesn't have a chance with you, why fuck with us like this?"

Anger replaced sadness as seconds ticked by, counting down the moments before, yet again, Sonia and I were ripped from one another. I couldn't care less if Tallia heard, or what she thought of me. "She's wasting her time and ours. Who does that?"

"Someone who thinks I'm being blinded by old feelings of a dead relationship that should stay buried."

"Fuck what she thinks," I said. "You told her your wishes, and she blatantly disregarded them."

"Baby," Sonia said, lifting my chin to plant a kiss on my lips. "It's not good-bye. She'll see I'm a waste of her time, and she'll send me to the wellness retreat."

"Promise me?" I asked. Because I couldn't tell her good-bye again and mean it. My heart refused to comply with any more good-byes when it came to her.

"I promise." Sonia began to let go, and my whole body begged her not to. The absence of her arms wrapped tightly around me made me feel strikingly cold. "Before we know it, we'll be at home, watching the dogs play. This will all be over. We'll be together."

She kissed the top of my head and walked with me out of the villa.

The top of my head tingled as tears wound down my cheeks. I

clung to her as she walked me to the black SUV waiting for Renee and me.

I climbed into the SUV's back row. Sonia kept my hand in hers, maintaining connection, as she pressed her body against the car's exterior to reach me. Toren pushed the middle seat back into place as Renee walked toward the vehicle.

"I love you, Elly Straus," Sonia said. Tears made her eyes sparkle, reflecting the car's interior light. "I crossed an ocean for you, a couple miles won't change shit, okay?"

I gave a nod. "Please..." I heard myself beg of Sonia, despite the others.

The car pulled out of the driveway, into the dark, and away from the villa's lights.

Away from Sonia, my light.

CHAPTER TWENTY-ONE

Elly

Toren, Heidi, and I sat circled around a dead firepit under the gazebo nearest our rooms at the wellness retreat. I didn't see much when we came in the night before, except that the property kept going and going beyond the darkness.

Now, in the light of day, I saw my assumptions had been correct.

The drive had taken more than ten minutes, but less than thirty. I didn't wear a watch, and without a phone I did a crappy job at keeping track of time. I could have looked at the SUV's dashboard, but time wasn't where my head had been.

I wished I knew how far a drive Sonia was from me. What she was doing at the moment.

My legs, covered in my exploding red pj's, were tucked into me on the outdoor chair. Summer mornings here were warm and comfortable, a lot like home. Before my coffee, I already needed shade and appreciated cool breezes.

I clutched my arms around my knees, not because of temperature. I felt shaky, scared, and thrown. I had expected this morning to go differently. Our first day after the villa, Sonia and I were going to wake up at a wellness retreat in each other's arms, find coffee after we decided to stumble out of bed, and then spend the day soaking up whatever wellness was offered. It had been too long since Sonia and I attended a yoga class together, laughing as we failed at contorting our bodies.

Like a cruel joke played on me by fate, I yet again experienced Sonia withdrawal. Time operated as an illusion, and everything she had ever said, done, or implied found its way into my proverbial strainer to be picked apart and rinsed with worry.

"I just feel like that was all unfair," Toren said. Their head hung low, and they leaned forward to use a half-burnt twig to draw lines in the firepit's ash.

"I think the name of the game is unfair," Heidi responded.

I silently agreed.

Heidi looked sullen. "At least we can spread out here," she added, as though her search for a silver lining at least produced something. "Until there's another violet ceremony, there's just five of us for this whole place." She turned to take in the panoramic view of our surroundings as she gently ran her fingers across her collarbone where her mic necklace used to be.

We knew the round of contestants to leave the first night went home, not here. Not only were we informed, but it was a topic of discussion around the house. Keeping their on-show fate a secret wasn't as big a deal when the producers planned to bring in a new crop of sapphics before getting the actual dates started. So it made sense that the wellness retreat was so empty.

Oak trees dotted the grounds. Surrounding their bases and climbing their trunks, English ivy added lines, circles, and triangles of deeper greens to the landscape. Clay pots of rosemary, peppers, and tomatoes lined two corners of our gazebo.

When I left my room this morning to find my way to the gazebo, I noticed blue hydrangeas stood at each of the front two corners of the old two-story home I stayed in. It looked like a charming farmhouse from the outside but was refurbished inside as a sort of lodge with at least five complete bedroom-bathroom combos.

To me, the grounds looked like a mixture between a retreat center, a spa, and a metaphysical store. According to the woman at the front desk who gave us our key cards, the grounds included hotel-type rooms, a pool, soaking spas, saunas, firepits, meditation labyrinths, nature trails, a cafeteria, and a university-style indoor lecture hall with stadium seating. She said it used to be an old Spanish farming estate.

If I hadn't left Sonia behind, if I had only left the show's other contestants, I might have been happy to be kicked off so early in the dating show contest. What the front desk woman explained sounded like something I could use. The wellness center was what sold me when I signed the contracts to be on this show.

A lot had changed since I decided to be on a sapphic dating show in Spain. I had changed. Breaking Sonia's spell over me was no longer the intent I approached new experiences with. An unrequited desire to be near her no longer lived in the back of my head, nagging with the need to be understood.

I understood now. I could set my mental gymnastics down, having cracked the code. The lightness of knowing rather than questioning lifted my spirits, motivated me to think positively. At the same time, alarms pulsed and blared through me. Memories of having Sonia ripped from me, in an instant, and being forced to go on without her, hung like a heavy storm cloud threatening to burst. It felt too reminiscent of our past.

"Where do you think they're keeping the coffee, and when do you think they'll bring out the relationship coaches?" I asked our little group, determined to not become a mopey bag of blues.

A breeze picked up, forcing the string of chakra flags hanging on the beam above me to dance. I always loved chakra flags. They reminded me of the rainbow Pride flag, another way to interpret and then symbolize the complex layers of humanity.

"*God*," Michelle groaned, walking through the circle of loose stones to enter the gazebo. "I hope we don't have to listen to relationship coaches. I'm good, thanks." She sat in an empty chair.

"I need a therapist, not a relationship coach," Toren muttered.

My inner mental health nerd almost raised my hand, but no, not the place. And also, not ethical.

"What do you think they're doing right now?" Toren asked the group.

This was eating Toren up. An urge to place a gentle hand on

their arm pushed me to raise my arm to touch them, but then I placed it back around my knees. I didn't know how they felt about touch, and this wasn't the moment to ask.

And what was I thinking anyway? My shaky touch would probably have made their anxiety worse. Transference of panic and all.

"Today is day..." Heidi paused. "I think it's day six, right?"

No one gave her the confirmation she wanted. Heidi waited a couple breaths and then kept on with her assumption. "Yeah, so, that probably means they're going to start a new round of group and one-on-one dates."

"I think Madrid Pride starts soon, doesn't it?" Michelle asked. "Sucks we can't look shit up still."

"You're right," Heidi said, nodding, the glimmer of new light in her blue eyes. "I forgot about that. The biggest Pride event, a week long, is in a week." She sat up a little straighter, likely with thoughts that were anything but straight.

"I wonder if their dates will be Pride related," Toren suggested. "Because that would be so epic." They lowered their chin and spoke into their chest. "And yet again, I'm missing it."

"We're still getting to celebrate," I reminded them. Because it was one of those threads of hope I held on to.

Getting to be a part of something as grand and inviting and affirming as Madrid Pride was a dream come true. Getting to be a part of it with Sonia was a whole other level. "I think it's on day fifteen because the finale, when Tallia decides who she's pursing a relationship with, is filmed on day sixteen. It's also the day that those who don't make it to the finale fly home." Rowdy was scheduled to be at his doggy sitter's until the seventeenth day, just in case I made it to the finale. I had it counted down on the planner they didn't let me bring.

I couldn't wait to hold him again, hear his happy *Mama's home!* grunts, and smell his comforting Rowdy scent. I had always felt bad for pugs and told myself I'd never have one, so as not to perpetuate their breeding. And then I met Sonia and her little girl, Harriet.

Until Harriet, I did not know a dog could embody so much snuggly undying insistent devotion. I did not know I needed a pug.

So, when a coworker told me about a sweet little brown and black pug baby that needed to be rehomed, I arranged to meet him later that same day. The little guy had no idea how badly I needed him. Neither did I.

Soon, I promised myself, *you'll be watching Harriet and Rowdy play, and this will all be worth it.*

Toren gave an appreciative nod. "I wonder who else will get kicked off between now and then," they added.

Heidi stood and stretched. She looked at me. "Yeah, I think I'm going to go look for coffee too."

I stood, inspired by her assumption of my earlier intentions, which now became my new intent.

For three days I woke up hoping to see Sonia and went to sleep disappointed.

On day one, I knew Sonia and I were going to be together. Day two's breath workshop exhumed a couple doubts I spent the rest of the day and part of the night wrestling. Yes, Sonia had promised to never blindside me again, but what if she couldn't follow through on that vow? Because she had made a vow before that she shattered when she broke up with me. How could I trust she wouldn't do it again?

Considering the possibility wasn't pleasant. But while at the wellness retreat, I realized it was a real possibility. I could only control me. I had the choice to extend my heart to Sonia after she broke my trust once. If I chose to do it, I couldn't blame her if she repeated her behavior. I would go in knowingly. Which would make a second betrayal like that from her more earth-shattering than the first.

At the villa, we'd agreed to try again. We decided on boundaries to begin with, ways to make sure we each felt safe. We came up with parameters for our future arguments and our future emotional check-ins, to ensure we stayed intentional with one another and didn't slip into complacency. We valued one another and, after time apart, knew we would do whatever it took to never have to be apart again.

If after our talks at the villa—and the talks I hoped we'd have at the wellness center, and back home—she still called me one day and told me things were over between us, I'm not sure I'd be able to ever trust someone with my heart again.

On the morning of day three, I exited my room onto the path leading to what we dubbed *our gazebo*, excited for my next breath work session.

In the days spent roaming the property since arriving, we'd located two more buildings of sleeping quarters, both slightly smaller than the one our rooms were in. Each building had its own gazebo. We were the only guests at the wellness center so far.

Mary, the relationship coach on staff, turned out to be pretty phenomenal. Even Toren liked her. Probably because, as Mary put it, "Our relationship with ourself is the most important relationship of all, and the most foundational."

I agreed, except when she left out the importance of the first six years of life, and the role of core caretakers in the emotional development of the human brain. But I understood and appreciated her point.

I appreciated it all, in fact. The twice a day yoga classes, private and group meditation sessions, Reiki sessions, vegan cafeteria, and Mary. But it did little to distract me from thinking about Sonia, wondering what she was doing, how she was feeling.

Back home in Spokane, I never did get over thinking about her, wondering what she was up to, secretly hoping to run in to her, but was also terrified to see the disgusted expression on her face when she saw me.

This time, missing her felt all kinds of better.

I spent my days trying new fruit smoothies and tofu dishes, stretching in child's pose and downward dog, inwardly excited to introduce it all to Sonia when she finally arrived.

Last night, while lying awake in bed, hoping she looked at the moon and thought of me the way I did her, I decided to trust this.

Not trust that Sonia would always be who I needed and wanted, but that my love would bring what I needed and wanted. As long as my love for myself was nourishing and intentional, I could trust my heart to make the right choices *in* love.

"Okay, here's what I think she meant." Toren sat back confidently in their chair in our gazebo and stretched their arms out before bringing their fingers to a triangle on their lap. "Tallia said, *I would have liked to have gotten to know you better, but others in this house have different values.*"

I sat beside Heidi.

Toren raised an index finger to no one in particular. "She wanted to get to know me better. And if she *could* have, she *would* have. But other people got in the way. On our date." Toren took a sip of tea and then their focus shifted beyond the gazebo.

I turned to see who they were looked at behind me and spotted Renee coming to join us with two mugs of coffee. This had become our morning ritual since the first morning, when I had gone looking for her and found not only Renee, but the self-serve coffee stand, with Renee beside it, enjoying a brew.

For as irritating as everyone said Renee was, I liked her. Sure, she had a chip on her shoulder. She was also kind and thoughtful. In my opinion she used a macho bravado to mask something tender, buried maybe deeper than even she could access. But as a person she was pretty fantastic.

I accepted my drink and thanked my new friend. She sat in the empty chair beside me. As usual, she looked sharp.

"I think that's plausible," I said.

Toren gave a nod. "Thank you."

"Hey," a familiar voice called from behind me.

I craned my neck to see who.

LeeAnn walked toward our gazebo, her arms open like she was going to hug someone. She spotted me and swerved sideways enough to enter the gazebo near me. I didn't stand and found myself on the receiving end of an awkward armpit-in-my-face hug.

They had an elimination last night. Hope cracked open like an egg in my chest. I peered in all the different directions. Was Sonia here?

Michelle swung her first-floor door open and bolted down the path for us. "You guys had a ceremony?" she yelled, as though it was a good thing.

For us, though, it was.

"Who else is here?" Michelle asked frantically, surveying where people were hiding as though her head was on a swivel. "How many did she vote off this time?"

She looked how I felt.

Michelle paused long enough for LeeAnn to pull away from me, stand to her full height, and answer.

"Three of us," LeeAnn answered. "They put us in a house smaller than this one, a little farther back." She pointed at the refurbished farmhouse we stayed in. "Heather and Sonia."

I jumped from my chair and ran down the path, past our building, toward the back of the property. I passed olive shrubs and oak trees, moving quicker down the path the more out of sight from the others I got.

Sonia was here. With me.

I had Sonia again.

Nothing else mattered.

Did anything else matter outside of the way Sonia's skin felt against mine? The way her eyes worshipped and lusted after me in a golden fiery gaze?

I made it to the next house back from mine and studied the three doors on the first level. If the building was remodeled like the one I was staying in, the second level room doors were in the back, at the tops of stairs.

I couldn't knock on all the doors.

Actually, I could.

I was considering which to start with first when Heather came from around back. "Good morning, stranger," she said with a wave.

She didn't head for me, but away from me, toward the path to our gazebo. "Where's the coffee?" she asked, motioning to the mug I carried.

I almost asked what she was talking about but realized I

clutched the empty cup. I must have spilled the coffee on my run. "Follow the path you're on, and you'll see a gazebo with the rest of us. They can show you."

"Awesome," Heather said, a hand in the air, not actually facing me.

"Wait!" I thought to ask. "Where's Sonia staying?"

"Bottom right," Heather answered without looking.

I ran across the grass to lean my body on her door. I exhaled and knocked.

She didn't say come in. She stood in the suddenly open doorway, her frame the most beautifully built piece of art. She wore dark blue joggers and a black T-shirt. I wrapped my arms around her midsection, and she lowered hers to embrace me, my chin at her heart. Comforting warmth encased my being, lulling me to take safe harbor in her.

I closed my eyes to keep the tears from burning so badly. I needed to feel her more, feel more of her. I shifted and wrapped my hands around the back of her neck, feeling her strength beneath my forearm. I tilted my face up to hers. Her perfect smile grew until her eyes smiled too.

I missed being the one who contributed to her happiness. It made my heart burst with a proud kind of love. I got to be the one. Her one.

But that was years ago. Now we stood on the threshold of our past and our future, in the moment of now.

Oh, how I wished we could live in the now, always. I wished that, like the song I sang on karaoke night, we could be together where our unfixable problems didn't matter. Where our friends didn't hate one another for breaking each other's hearts. Where the angry after-breakup thoughts were washed away like an etched heart in the sand at high tide.

Did she know how deeply I felt these things for her? How she still lived in my bones and I hoped to God I still lived in hers?

"I missed you," she said into my hair on an exhale.

Sonia pulled away and placed her hands at each side of my

face. She tilted my head up to look into my eyes. Her thumb began to graze the bottom of my jaw before she pulled it back.

Her happy smile, the one I gave her, faded as she sighed.

I cocked my head. "What's wrong?"

Chapter Twenty-two

Sonia

"Nothing's wrong," I said, wishing I could pull Elly closer somehow, breathe her in deeper.

Elly looked up to me and raised a light brown eyebrow in question.

Shutting the door, I pulled her onto my lap on the bed. "Oh, I missed this." I pressed my lips to the center of her forehead, one of my favorite spots on her body to kiss. "It's nothing bad. I'm excited. I get to see you, go to Madrid Pride with you, and then go home with you. Talk about the perfect end to this trip."

I'd finished making my bed and was about to put on my black Adidas when I heard yelling outside. The fact that she found me before I could find her made me chuckle and love her a little bit more.

"Well actually," I said playfully, changing my tone to show as much, "there is this one thing. It's been eating me alive since you left the villa."

Elly scrambled off my lap and sat cross-legged across from me on the bed. Her smile tightened. A glaze of tears amplified her eyes.

I couldn't mess with her, it was too soon, not like this. I dropped the ruse. "Baby, no, don't worry. I'm sorry, that was too soon."

"Well, say it already," Elly urged, my apology doing nothing to melt her rigidness.

I laughed, feeling bad for how cute I thought she looked. "Can people call us Son-Ell again? Or should we change that up?" I asked. *Sonia* meant meadow and *Elly* meant moonlight. We used to say we went together like a moonlit meadow.

Elly laughed and playfully gave a slap to my forearm. "Sonia Comstock, don't you ever do that to me again. My nerves are too shot."

My heart smiled along with my lips. I loved when she used my name like that, a mostly play scolding, the way her lips moved when she slowly pronounced my last name. She scooted to close the inches between us and wrapped an arm around my shoulders. I leaned my head in to her.

"Can we be done going nights and days without talking?" I asked. "Done for the rest of our days?"

Elly's presence made everything in my life brighter, lighter, happier. She brought meaning to the otherwise meaningless. The villa, without her, could have been a tiny shack as far as I was concerned. I had the chance to walk Madrid's famous park, and I kept thinking about Manito Park with Elly. Because even at night, flowers bloomed brighter and smelled sweeter with her around.

The air around Elly had an effect on me, as though she changed the ratio of oxygen to other gasses in the atmosphere and made me high from exposure. I wanted to be high on Elly the rest of my life.

When so many parts of living in this world were hard, why wouldn't I want for her as many things as possible that felt right? If I could contribute to her happiness, I would.

"You know what?" I said, flattening my lap enough to pull the folded journal paper from my pocket. "I have wanted to read this to you since day one." I unfolded the thick paper.

"What is it?" she asked, leaning over to view what the paper contained.

"I wrote a poem to you," I answered. "Months ago. When I saw you, that poem came to mind. It wasn't the only one I wrote about you, about us, but for some reason it was the one I couldn't forget. After brunch that first day, I looked for you, and when I couldn't find you, I used the time to write as much of the poem as I could remember. I wanted to give it to you. I don't always know the right things to say. But when given the opportunity, my hands somehow do know."

"You write poems now?" she asked. "Could you be any more perfect?"

She leaned into me and settled in. "I can't wait, baby."

I took that as the cue to begin. Nervousness fluttered my heart and shook my hands. My poems never saw the light of day. They were for me and me only. Except for Elly's. She needed to know how I felt, deserved to know. I cleared my throat.

"Okay, ugh. Okay." With an inhale, I focused on the first line and began. "Oh, it's called 'I-90.'" I cleared my throat again, to begin.

"It happens sometimes, to the best of us,
The loss of words and explanations.
The inability to express the rush.
A highway we've traveled a thousand million times,
Littered with axles and bumpers,
Jammed up from side to side.
The path of communication,
My heart to my head, my head to my mouth,
A treacherous obstacle course
With no quick way out.
I admit, I could have told you as much.
Cried for help as emotions crashed and the ability to
        regulate flew from my clutch.
You'd witnessed tears shed before that fateful day.
You were the keeper of my secret weaknesses,
Out of anyone, you knew my heart beat for you,
And that's how it would stay.
But my mouth didn't open to speak,
Your ear didn't try to hear.
Promises twisted like metal,
Turned our route into a burial yard.
A rust pile created from tears."

I folded the paper into itself before daring a glance at Elly. Her brown eyes softened, sparkling in the lamplight like glowing embers. A fireless flame ignited in her eyes.

Tears sprang to mine.

I leaned in to gently place a kiss upon her full lips and pulled away to look into her gaze.

"Thank you," she said on a breath. She wrapped her arms around my neck and drew me in, to crush our bodies together. "I love you so much. Thank you for that. I'll always treasure it." She pressed her mouth to mine. Our fingers twisted through hair and clung to one another's backs as we kissed life into each other.

As though we were substance and starving at the same time, pure passion pulsed in the moment, our bodies moving with its beat. I barely noticed my shirt being lifted over my head. If it led to my body being closer to hers, I wanted it.

So badly I wanted to reacquaint myself with the dip in her collarbone, with the curves of her neck. To trail my fingers and lips across her smooth as silk skin. She raised her arms as I worked to get her shirt onto the floor. I unlatched her bra with a quickness before we struggled to peel my sports bra from my body.

Our laughter at the reminders of awkward struggles didn't last long before our mouths were busy again.

We could have devoured one another with hunger, famished for each other's touch, kiss, taste. As though we had survived in the desert to finally stumble upon an oasis and knew enough to embrace it for the life-giving fulfillment it brought.

The life force and life source of pure, genuine love.

I doubted anything more powerful existed in the world.

Elly's kisses left my lips to trail my jaw, my neck, and down to my breasts. Her hand fit each breast just the way I remembered. I needed more than her touch. I needed the warmth of her tongue.

I grabbed her ponytail with one hand and trailed the other down her back as her mouth found my nipple.

Seconds after my moan escaped, Elly landed a hard, passionate kiss on my mouth. With her free hand, she worked to rid me of my joggers. I helped her release the last pants leg as she lowered her body.

Her lips and fingers returned to a territory they knew well, as she walked them down the line of my stomach. I inhaled sharply as my abs tightened and squirmed under her mouth. Against my control, my pelvis pushed toward her, vying for her tongue.

She pressed her mouth into me, muffling her chuckle, teasing me with her hot breath. I heard myself whine. I wanted her. In fact, I wanted her to know how desired she truly was. How many nights I thought of her between my legs when I touched myself.

Her flexed lean shoulders and shaved undercut was the only view I wanted between my legs.

How I missed her between my legs.

Elly's mouth dipped down as she slid her tongue between my legs and back up again with flat pressure. I moaned. As much as my neck was tempted to give out, I couldn't not watch her as she went to work, her biceps shifting, her neck flexing with each directional change of her tongue.

My fingers found her hair and wrapped through blond tresses.

Elly's lapping sped in pace and strength, building me the way only she knew how. If I could have grabbed her hair and felt her tongue between my legs and also dug my nails into her back and plunged my tongue into her mouth, I would have.

I wanted all of her, in every way, at the same time. To fill myself with her and empty myself into her.

"Elly," I whispered into the cozy room, finally with the one person I wanted. Her touch, it brought life to my body, awoke a passion only she had the ability to summon, as though I was alive with more than my own being.

My muscles tightened with growing pleasure. Elly quickened and lightened her pressure, bringing my body to a more heightened state, as though my nerve endings neared the surface of my skin in search of her.

My pelvis tilted, seeking her mouth.

She crushed into me, her tongue unspooling pleasure from me.

Awake and hungry for what she had to give, my body complied, my hips gyrating under her squeezing hands.

Until I couldn't control them anymore. Until my hips squeezed to contain the growing orgasm, tightening with each new level Elly brought me to.

My fingertips pressed into her scalp.

My thighs shook uncontrollably.

My shoulders shoved into the pillow, jerking my pelvis up, reaching the top of the roller coaster Elly took me on. She grabbed my hips tightly and put me in place without missing a beat.

Fireworks of pleasure exploded between my legs, in the depths of my belly, curling my toes, and tingling my teeth. "Elly," I screamed into the ether, thankful.

"Elly," I said again, tears streaming down my face as my pelvis lowered and my emotions replaced pleasure. I rolled to my side, and she curled around me.

She covered me. Her arms pulled me into her and squeezed my back to her chest. She wrapped her leg around mine and melded me into her.

Tears rolled down my temple onto the sheet beside her chest. She ran a hand over my hair.

"I'm so glad I get to have you, baby," she whispered into the dark, quiet room. I lived to feel the vibration of her chest when she spoke. To be that close to her, to be able to hear her heartbeat, her breath.

I inhaled and smiled, breathing her in, high on Elly. Hearing her voice call me *baby* melted my core. I helped her position herself to lie beside me, her head on my chest, my arm around her shoulder.

When I arrived in Spain, I was a different person. This experience changed me in ways I had a feeling I would be unpacking for a while. In a sense, I came for the fantasy, for the elaborate dates, grand gestures, and stomach butterflies.

I got them all too.

What I hadn't considered before, or maybe I had and just didn't understand the difficulty, was that every coin had at least two sides. No person or situation was only one thing. To truly love someone was not the same as loving for the fantasy of it all. Loving the fantasy was loving only one side of the coin, the side that best benefitted the receiver. Loving realistically, truly, was to love the whole coin, the whole person.

To love myself when I wasn't feeling one hundred percent. Taking comfort not in the fact that I was capable of giving one hundred percent, but in knowing however much I gave was given with heart. To love Elly's whole self and choose to assume the best of her, even when my insecurities insisted otherwise. To see the hard days for what they were and know brighter days would come.

I hoped when we got home, Elly and I would fit just as well, if not better, than before. But we wouldn't know until we tried, until we practiced our new intentions through daily choices. That part, I was excited about.

"Do you think we've learned our lesson, enough, that it'll work this time?" I asked earnestly on a relaxed sigh. "Because I very much do."

It took Elly a few breaths to answer. "Both of us have learned. Speaking in flower terms," she started.

I laughed. That was a thing I used to say, *speaking in flower terms*, because she had a way of comparing life's lessons to flowers, or basically everything to plants.

"Okay good, that landed right," she said before kissing me on my chest, closest to where her head lay. "I didn't want you to think I was mocking you or anything. I missed you saying it. And, hey, Manito Park was never the same without you. Especially the rose gardens. I missed having someone to say all my witty metaphors to."

My exhale felt as though it was the chill leaving a cavernous void within me that held the emptiness of missing Sonia. I could fill it with her now, joking with her, planning with her, gossiping with her, my best friend and lover. No more violet ceremonies to keep us apart.

"It landed very well," I said. "Like a dandelion seed lands in fertile soil after a gust separates the fluffy white umbrella."

Her chuckle warmed my skin. "So, speaking in flower terms."

I laughed and tickled the highest side of her naked hip.

She sank more into me. "I think we've both learned that we don't have to choose which flower to be, which way to show up in the world. And for us, as women, we're given flower options, by the way."

"I see," I said.

"Yeah," Elly went on. "We know we don't have to choose now. For instance, I can be a violet with thorns."

"Are you saying you feel like you're a violet with thorns and that should be okay?" I asked. "Because it is. We all have different aspects of ourselves."

"That's exactly it," Elly said.

I exhaled a sigh. "I missed listening to how you think."

"Some violets have thorns," she went on. "We don't all have to be a certain type of flower. We don't have to take on the flower's characteristics and hide the rest, the ones that don't fit. We're more than our appearance and the scent others perceive our fragrance to be. Why fit neatly into one type or another? Some of us are spliced, pieced together. I may be a violet, but not all my petals are purple. And also, I have thorns. The balance of it all is accepting myself while not jabbing you in the process. I think you've come to similar conclusions."

I imagined flowers as people, interacting with thorns and hidden beauty, navigating a world where each was different and found fascinating and wonderful for it.

I rolled to my side and shared a pillow with Elly. "I do have similar conclusions," I said, ending the statement with a kiss.

"And I'm not saying we don't have a lot of talking still to do," she said, her eyes smiling, inches from my own. When her eyes were happy, she glowed—her voice, her skin, her touch, all glowed. "We have a lot to catch up on, to relearn each other. I know we've both changed and stayed the same. And we'll take our time unpacking everything."

"That sounds perfect," I said. "I want to be in your life. I want to spend dinners with you and hear about your day and what you think about the world. I want to pick you up and take you to the lake. I want us to take the dogs out for a picnic at the park. I want the simple things with you. I want you in my life."

"I'm so excited to go home now," she said on sigh as she nuzzled into my neck. "I'm in Spain saying I want to go back to Spokane." She laughed. "Never thought that would happen."

"We just need to get through these next few days," I said.

She wrapped an arm and a leg around me.

"In a few days, there will be a violet ceremony. The next day is the all-contestant Pride party. We get through that, and we're on a plane home, picking up the dogs and cuddling in one of our beds for a week." It sounded like heaven.

"I'm all in," Elly cooed. "There's stuff I want to show you here." She paused. "And also plenty of other ways to pass the time. Making up for lost time and all."

"Speaking in flower terms, that is," I added.

Elly responded with a kiss.

❖

Last summer, I loathed the idea of seeing Elly at Spokane Pride. There were too many unknowns and raw emotions between us, that I couldn't think of a scenario where seeing her wouldn't feel like fresh heartbreak.

Now we stood on the corner of connecting streets, people weaving around us, celebrating at Madrid Pride together.

I couldn't help but smile when Elly put her outfit on this morning. Yesterday she had admitted to bringing two Pride outfits, just in case the weather changed or her confidence sputtered. Today she was feeling confident in her faded jean cutoff shorts and rainbow knitted crop top.

I wore a pair of midthigh navy-blue shorts to go with her white tank, and an open button-up white shirt covered in artistic rainbows, to match her top. When we looked in the mirror before heading out this morning, she said my white Adidas pulled my outfit together, and I didn't disagree.

Elly presented herself in a way that made me drool. How she

pulled together the colors and fits of her creative outfits, how she matched them with her usually wooden accessories and smelled edible with essential oils. I didn't care if she wore a hippie skirt or booty shorts. If her hair was in a morning droopy ponytail or curled, cascading down her back for a night out. Who she was wouldn't change. She would always take pride in her appearance and carry herself with the confidence she created within herself.

To me, she would always be sexy.

After two poetry readings, one meal, who knew how many art booths, and one partial concert, Sapphire, Toren, Katy, Elly, and I shuffled from what felt like a huge block party to a quieter side street. Our group consisted of the nerdy readers in the villa, which was how the group formed and started the day with poetry readings.

One thing led to another, and now we congregated, deciding what to do next. We all agreed to find cold Jell-O shots or just any beverages consisting of chill and alcohol. We walked toward an active street in search of empty outdoor patio seating attached to a restaurant or bar.

"There's a lesbian bar here," Sapphire squealed, studying her map as we passed tables of people socializing. "Just one more street over. I'm gonna let the others know we're heading there, in case anyone wants to meet up."

"That's the little lesbian bar we hit on the group date, called Fulanita de Tal," Elly said to only me.

I squeezed her hand and gave a devilish grin. "From the way you made it sound, we can't leave without getting you in a corner there." I motioned my head to the bar.

She smacked me and shook her head. It wasn't a no.

"I'm going to wait in line while you find a spot for us to sit. What do you all want to drink?" Katy asked.

We gave our drink orders and wove through the massive crowd in such a tiny space.

Just then, three women stood and left a blue metal table and folding chairs. We filled their spots before the metal had a chance to cool. Fans propped in corners and hanging from the ceiling kept air flowing through the cramped space. But not enough.

When Katy found us, Michelle and LeeAnn were with her, helping her carry drinks. I handed Elly her lemon drop before accepting my rum and Coke and wrapping my hands around the cold glass.

Elly and I nursed our cold drinks, side by side, while we watched a reality dating show live at our table. LeeAnn and Sapphire openly avoided one another, no longer attempting to pretend they hadn't been involved in a villa tryst. Tallia and Shay had been MIA since we all arrived and parted ways. Which made Toren antsy, anxious to complete their grand gesture plan as a last ditch for Tallia. Sapphire helped Toren recover—they were open about being exes since Sapphire arrived at the wellness retreat.

Out of everyone, I figured I would stay connected to a couple people, definitely Beth. Elly said she and Sapphire were forevermore best friends, so I expected Sapphire in my life too. But I had my friend group back home, people I went to school with and others I had met between then and now. They were a lot less drama, basically a lot less of everything. They were known, supportive, home.

And then there was Elly. If my friends were home, she was my hearth.

I eyed Elly, winked, and finished my drink. She smiled and slurped the rest of hers down.

"I have to pee," I announced, flashing a huge grin at Elly.

She stood, fixing her short shorts.

"I remember where it's at. Follow me," she said.

I gave an exasperated look around the bar, flashed a grin to Beth, and pretended to dive into the sea of people toward the restrooms after Elly.

Only second in line outside the bathroom door, it wasn't long before we got entrance. Elly's eyes caught mine with…was that a challenge? It had been a while since she had given me that look. I wasn't sure if that was still what it meant.

I smirked back. A stall opened up and she went in, giving me a wink before shutting her door. I had planned to invite myself into her stall, push Elly up against a stall wall, and cup her breast in my hand, my mouth on hers.

Her halter top practically begged me to move the fabric aside and release her beautiful breasts.

But I was playful and that felt too easy, too expected. When she had told me about this place, and her fantasy of what she would do to me here, I secretly planned to give her the exact scenario. To switch things up and surprise her.

A stall opened for me and I did my business. When I exited to wash my hands, Elly's stall no longer showed her Converse under the door and she wasn't at the sinks either.

I left the bathroom, hoping to find her waiting right outside, when a hand caught my wrist and pulled me back deeper into the club, to a separate room full of techno music and dancing bodies. Black walls intensified the strobe lights.

Elly urged me into a small corner alcove, where the strobes barely touched. Music bumped, people laughed. Our bodies slowly began moving together to the beat of their own sensual, intimate drum.

How many times had we been out in the past and found private moments among the crowds to create a bubble of us? It had been so long, that now I relished every tantalizing second like it was a dream come true.

Elly attacked. Her mouth found mine in the most delicious, hunger-filled way. I grabbed at her ponytail, seeking to run fingers through loose strands.

My right hand moved down to cup her breast, and she leaned her head back to rest against the wall with a moan. My lips pressed into the skin exposed on her chest, pushing her breast up enough to kiss the flesh above the crochet.

Oh, how I wished I could get on my knees, pull her shorts to the side…

But that would be the opposite of hot for her. I walked my fingers down past the waistband on her shorts, not messing with the button, until I reached flesh again. Gliding the back of my knuckles along her inner thigh line, my fingers found themselves under the fabric of her shorts, nearing between her legs.

"Baby," she whispered loudly. She brought her head up to look me in the eyes. The dark want of sensual dreams pulsed in her gaze. "I want you so bad."

The back of my hand rested on her inner thigh as two fingers ventured farther. Her warm wetness greeted me. I allowed my fingers to slide around in small circles, feeling another part of Elly I had missed dearly. When she tensed just enough, I shifted from slow circles to sliding up and down over her clit, urging it to swell and grow.

Her lips quivered, and I neared my ear to her mouth, to hear those sweet sounds of pleasure I missed—the way her breath caught when I changed speeds, how she begged me for more, the way she would soon try to say my name on shaky breaths.

I found her mouth with mine again as I quickened my pace, my hand shifting into short, precise, intent movements.

"You've got me, baby," I assured her as her back tensed and arched under my free hand.

"I…" she started to say before a moan froze her tense body in place.

I kept my pace and motion, my fingers soaked and set on nothing but Elly's rising pleasure, my own growing in response.

"I love you," she called out. "Don't stop, baby, don't stop!"

Building up for her grand finale, I shoved her over the edge into pure bliss. She teetered on the brink of falling over, her muscles flexed, her mouth open, ready to yell when the incoming wave hit.

My lips found the side of her neck and bit down before saying, "I love you too, Elly."

Her body jerked and sent her sailing. Her head fell back as she yelled out in pleasure, where no one could hear her screams. Bodies ground all around us. Music pulsed. Lights strobed.

Elly fell toward me, resting her head on my shoulder. "We've never done that," she said on an exhale with a smile.

The two of us held one another in the tight hidden alcove, lovers continually clinging to each other as though here in Spain we could live in our own cave of wonders. We could keep the world out, hidden among the commotion.

THE TELL ALL

Sonia

"Hello, and welcome back to *The Sapphic Bacheloress's Tell All*," Kamal announced from the chair at the head of our triangle of seats.

The show's set looked like a large living room, orphaned from its house. Mismatched couches and oversized chairs created two lines converging at the point, where Kamal sat to observe us all, his shoulders back and head high.

His pointed smile scanned the contestants. His gaze passed over Elly and me on our mint green love seat, only to return with a mischievous grin. "Your turn in the hot seat, you two."

I gave Elly's left shoulder a squeeze, my arm over my girlfriend's bare back. Elly returned the squeeze to my hand in hers, clasped on her thigh. We were not naive to the real purpose of reality show tell alls. If the show's season was a tube of toothpaste, the tell all was the producer's last-ditch effort to roll the tube as tightly as needed to squeeze out any untapped drama left.

Thankfully, five months ago I had entered this contest with the personal intent of not doing or saying anything I didn't want revealed in the tell all. The first few episodes of the season had aired, and we were all on a social media blackout until today's filming aired.

When we returned home from Spain, Elly and I couldn't be seen together in public, lest our love give away a piece of the show's dramatic ending. We didn't mind the privacy to reconnect, and when we felt ready to include our closest friends and family, we hosted phone-free house karaoke parties and game nights.

Today, while on set in what looked like a New York City warehouse from the outside, I couldn't wait to be seen publicly holding my love's hand, kissing her, matching outfits with her.

Our outfits matched, intentionally. My forest-green button-up matched the flowy fabric of her dress, which I dubbed my new favorite forest-fairy outfit of hers. Pink fabric roses dotted her skirt, as though they bloomed along the vine and leaf stitching. Beneath the tulle, light pink satin reached up her torso. Green lace covered and accentuated her breasts in a plummeting neckline.

This particular dress she'd picked out with me beside her, on a recent trip to Seattle, for today's filming. Although we had acted like friends in public and wore beanies in the cold weather to obscure our identities, the act of planning for the future with Elly made it all worth it. I had missed those little things no one would have given a second thought to—being in Elly's inner circle, being a part of not just what she presented to the world, but also her process of preparing for the world. Just like being able to see Elly in her rainbow glasses before her official day began.

"Sonia and Elly." Kamal spoke to the camera. "Other than the bacheloress and her lucky partner, Shay, these two have stolen our hearts the most and left us wanting so much more," Kamal jokingly whined. He fixed his sad expression and motioned to the big screen TV onstage, standing at the base of the triangular seating setup. "Lucky for us, we've got secret footage! And I'm not talking about the hidden garden cameras, or the time you thought the confession room wasn't filming."

Elly and I squirmed under the crowd's laughter. She flashed a nervous glance at me before smiling at Kamal. I pressed a kiss into her forehead and the live audience clapped.

"We have"—Kamal drew the words out—"for your viewing and listening pleasure, Sonia and Elly's audio story."

Color splashed across the dark screen, forming the opening image to a video Elly made on our flight home from Madrid.

"On our way home!" Elly sang, wearing her light green lounge sweats, her hair up in a ponytail, showing off her shaved sides and lotus undercut.

If I was the bacheloress waiting at the front of the villa, and Elly had exited the limo to meet me for the first time, wearing her sweat lounge outfit and a ponytail, I would have gladly scooped her and nuzzled into the softness of her outfit, breathed in her mixture of scents—detergent, fabric softener, and essential oils.

"Last stop before home," I pretended to whine in the video, drudging through DFW before pepping up to wrap an arm around nearby Elly and pulling her close to kiss her on the temple. "Finally doing this with my one."

The video shifted views to a photo of *Circling* by Christopher Janney. More photos tumbled onto the screen and bounced away—the two of us standing in the center of the exhibit, pointing to an etched silver circle in the floor, and a closer image of the words in the silver. We wore the same travel outfits we flew to Spain in, freshly cleaned for the flight home.

What the viewers couldn't see from the photos, the truth behind our smiles, was our delight in knowing we had both visited the exhibit separately, thinking of one another. And on our return flight, we got to do it together. We got to medicate the wound created by doing something separately that we had intended to experience together.

When the screen flashed black and began filling with pictures of our arrival home, my low whisper poured from the speakers, background audio accompanying the happy photos of us hiking, at Gonzaga games, and in cuddle puddles with the dogs on the couch.

My voice uttered through the speakers, "God, she got even more gorgeous."

Heat exploded in my chest, lodging a thick tightness in my throat. They were using my mic audio from the show. I remembered thinking those words when I first saw Elly at the brunch, and again while sneaking glances from Tallia's table. I must have said the words out loud, under my breath, to no one.

Videos shot after we returned home to Spokane, of our dogs

first meeting and chasing one another around the backyard, began to play as mic recordings filled the background audio. I hadn't realized I'd said so many of my inner thoughts.

"Fuck me, she's there, in those damn glasses."

I remembered saying that to myself the first morning, when I came downstairs and saw Elly sitting there on the couch beside Sapphire.

"How did I make Elly's lemon drop? How did I…"

That audio clip had been recorded after I offered to get Tallia's drink, and she asked for Elly's favorite go-to. My talking to myself paused long enough for us to hear my breath and glasses clinging as I hurried around the kitchen in a panic to get back out to where Elly stood, to be in her presence again.

"No, she doesn't get Elly's version…"

When I made Elly a lemon drop, it always came with a drop of lavender oil.

"Bullshit," Elly's recorded voice uttered, and the audience laughed.

My stunt on the show—which I'd pulled to remind her of us, of how I used to make lemon drops for her, of how I ordered them at Kitty's when we went out—had clearly backfired. Elly and I had discussed this turn of events in the months we'd been home, but hearing Elly's fresh anger over the speakers made me smile.

We didn't always get it right with one another, but eventually we got it. And that's what mattered to me.

Kamal and our fellow contestants swooned over the TV. Elly pulled her gaze from the screen to see me staring at her with a smile. We locked eyes. I gave a nod. I would only ever make lavender lemon drops for Elly. No one else. This trip solidified that fact for both of us. Tears filled Elly's eyes.

Photos bounced onto the screen of us walking at night in Manito Park, despite the cold weather, in an attempt to be outside together with no one seeing. Harriet and Rowdy wore matching sweaters. We posed together, kissing on benches, under archways, and inside a gazebo.

"It was like you took a chunk of me, who I was, and didn't have the decency to even try to give remnants back. I didn't need to be left alone, Sonia. I needed you to try."

Frozen in the moment, we listened, for the first time, to what our mic necklaces picked up when we had forgotten about an audience and only saw one another. When we began back at the beginning.

"Goddamn it, Elly, you of all people should have known how grief works. How much do I have to give to get the grace your clients get?"

"Did you ever even love me?"

"Fuck, I never stopped!"

"You know, I still masturbate to you."

Laughs sprang from the audience, shifting the mood. Elly blushed and shook her head at me. I nodded with a proud smile, remembering the way my heart burst and my core yearned for her when she told me that little tidbit at the villa.

"There's no poem, no story, where we don't end up together, Elly Straus. It just doesn't exist."

"I wouldn't want to live in a world where there wasn't you, Sonia Comstock."

The audience offered swooning sounds as Elly laid her head on my shoulder. I pulled her closer to me on the love seat, wishing I could hold her on my lap, to have our bodies as near to one another as publicly appropriate. Her tears created a wet patch on the dark green shoulder of my button-up. I twisted my torso and neck enough to kiss the top of Elly's forehead.

We did it, baby, I wanted to whisper into her ear but decided the crowd had had enough of our private encounters. We didn't need to provide more. Soon, filming would wrap up, and we would fly home together, to our new life, intentionally built and maintained.

When our leases were up next year, we planned to combine households and start fresh once again, a new chapter in our combined story. Because *The Sapphic Bacheloress* wasn't our only opportunity to begin again. Every misstep, every miscommunication, every mistake, was a new chance to begin again in one way or another. A breath of new life to blow away doubts, the droplets of new rain to quench the drought.

Not every new chapter in the story of our love would be pleasant, we knew that much to be true. And yet the consistent stability and security of the good chapters, and those micromemories threaded throughout that meant the world to us, would keep us going strong.

I inhaled Elly's detergent and patchouli scent, felt her hair's blondish-brown flyways tickle my chin, and smiled. This woman beside me lived in my bones. It made sense that being hers, and knowing she was mine, settled my nerves and calmed my heart. Happiness flowed through my veins.

The photos flickering on and off the screen slowed until only one remained, our first ever picture taken together, the night we met at the sapphic prom in Seattle. A younger version of me stood nervously beside the smartest, most attractive woman I ever laid eyes on.

"Can we go home now and do better?" Elly's voice begged through the speaker, onto the stage, and into the audience. "Please?"

I remembered the exact moment this audio was captured. We had been walking out of our breath work session at the wellness center, the evening before our Madrid Pride outing. We had been walking the path from the main building to her room, strolling in the twilight hours, while the sun hung low in the sky, splashing oranges and purples across the horizon.

When she asked that, my heart felt like it had burst in the best of ways. In a low and throaty voice, on the brink of tears, I responded, "*God*, I've been waiting *a year* for you to ask that. Let's go home."

About the Author

Rachel Sullivan is a certified peer counselor and the author of feminist stories of love, in its many forms. She lives in the Pacific Northwest with her menagerie of pets and plants.

Books Available From Bold Strokes Books

The Moon to Me by Ana Hartnett. Sometimes it takes traveling thousands of miles to discover what's been yours all along. (978-1-63679-918-6)

Royal Rush: 75 Days to Fall in Love by Lissandra Rowe. When a royal matchmaking scheme leads to a chance encounter with Isabella Acosta-Ramon, a slow burn sparks that neither can deny. (978-1-63679-965-0)

To Love Violets for Their Thorns by Rachel Sullivan. Forced to face the heartbreak they never quite got over, Elly and Sonia must decide: breathe fresh life into an old love or try again with someone new? (978-1-63679-928-5)

Virtually Perfect by Melissa Sky. If your AI flirts better, listens harder, and never ghosts you...does that count as love? (979-8-90035-005-9)

Brooke Takes Queen by Alaina Erdell. Brooke Staley faces personal and professional upheaval when Elizabeth Bettancourt, the emotionally scarred new owner of the resort she works for, considers selling. (978-1-63679-886-8)

Coda by Anna Gram. Parker is intriguing, magnetic, impossible to ignore—and completely wrong for Hannah. But sometimes love's melody refuses to end. (978-1-63679-926-1)

The Debutante Dilemma by Jane Walsh. Two debutantes are engaged to wealthy and titled brothers...but discover they only have eyes for each other. (978-1-63679-896-7)

The Love Book by Gun Brooke. When literary agent Rowan Cross receives an anonymous manuscript that deeply resonates with her, Verity realizes she has accidentally sent her own manuscript, complete with her very real feelings for her boss! (978-1-63679-850-9)

Secrets Under the Junipers by Suzie Clarke. Who killed Hallie Lynn Peeples? Cecilia McConnel needs to know. Bitsy Hanover holds the key. Can love uncover secrets? (978-1-63679-845-5)

Traveling Toward Forever by Erin Dutton. When almost-strangers take a road trip through America's national parks, love may be the final destination. (978-1-63679-894-3)

Beautiful Things by Emma L McGeown. A warmhearted romance of missed chances, undeniable chemistry, and a stubborn love that maybe, just maybe, can find its way back. (978-1-63679-934-6)

The Great Popcorn Romance by Georgia Beers. Opposites attract, and Riley Shaw stands no chance of resisting Hannah Kramer's magnetic pull. But opposites know just how to drive each other crazy... (978-1-63679-910-0)

Love Takes a Village by Karis Walsh. As Lena Preiss struggles to manage a busy restaurant in the Bavarian Christmas village of Leavenworth, Washington, chocolatier Devin Meyer brings an unexpected richness into her life, along with her delicious desserts. (978-1-63679-902-5)

Secrets of the Heart by Jenny Frame. When a beautiful stranger starts asking questions about Nikki Sharkey, head of an infamous crime syndicate, Nikki will stop at nothing to protect her daughter Isla. (978-1-63679-653-6)

Talon and the Songbird by Julia Underwood. In a world where survival depends on strategic alliances, Makayla and Talon must navigate not only complex politics but also the dangerous territory of their hearts. (978-1-63679-970-4)

Three Blissful Days by Dena Blake. Kendall Jackson attempts to make her ex regret dumping her by announcing she's dating beautiful park ranger Ivy Patterson. But there's nothing fake about how attracted Ivy is to Kendall. (978-1-63679-707-6)

The Art of Love by Ali Vali. When Mimi and Bianca both set their sights on Jolly, sparks fly, loyalties are tested, and hearts collide as they navigate the unpredictable nature of their hearts. (978-1-63679-719-9)

Chasing Her Scent by MJ Williamz. When Sheridan Rousseau walks into Lisette Mouton's charming little bookstore in Quebec City, she unknowingly holds the key to a mysterious box hidden in a secret room. (978-1-63679-900-1)

Heart's Run by D. Jackson Leigh. Hoping to recover an escaped racing mare, stock transporter Tobie Mason locks horns with local wild horse advocate Maggie Wilkes. (978-1-63679-825-7)

Scandalous by Kris Bryant. When a Hollywood actress trades places with her twin sister, everyone's in an uproar about getting duped, but Lindsay's more concerned about finding out which twin she made out with. (978-1-63679-874-5)

The Secrets of Rhydian Hill by Ronica Black. A doctor in need of a new start. A woman running from a killer. A love story that could end in tragedy. (978-1-63679-880-6)

Feeling Lucky by Krystina Rivers. What happens when, despite suddenly having enough money to buy almost anything, Lucy and Tanner start to discover that maybe all they need is each other? (978-1-63679-876-9)

Iceberg by Gun Brooke. When Lady Arabella hires Zandra, she never expects to find love, especially not as a disaster looms on the horizon. (978-1-63679-908-7)

It Happened One Semester by Aurora Rey. After a Pride night hookup, can eager new Assistant Professor Hudson Greene and Dean of Advising Callie Shaw overcome the odds and ace falling in love? (978-1-63679-814-1)

It's Kind of a Bad Idea by Sarah G. Levine. What happens when an emotionally unavailable serial dater meets the one woman she can't help but fall for—who happens to be the one woman who told her not to? (978-1-63679-920-9)

Thankful for You by Tagan Shepard. Everyone deserves to find their person. Maybe Karen has finally found hers? (978-1-63679-884-4)

What Happens On Location by Nan Campbell. How can Helen produce a successful movie when its director is the woman responsible for the demise of her marriage? (978-1-63679-904-9)

When Love Comes Around by Radclyffe & Ronica Black. Can Maya Sanchez and Nolan Wright trust each other enough to build something real, or will the past tear them apart? (978-1-63679-930-8)

www.ingramcontent.com/pod-product-compliance
Lightning Source LLC
Chambersburg PA
CBHW030520020726
47494CB00004B/1167